AMIDST THE CASTLES

Amidst the Castles

JacQueline Vaughn Roe

ISBN: 978-1-950536-91-7

To my swan sister, Joy—
we will forever miss you

&

To my middle, Sydney—
I pray you will enjoy even the misadventures along the journey

RONA
Queen's Tower
King Purnell's Castle
Lord Colin
Sir Reginald
Castle of Silver Birds
Maer
Illyan Sea
Kabir Island
W
N
E
S

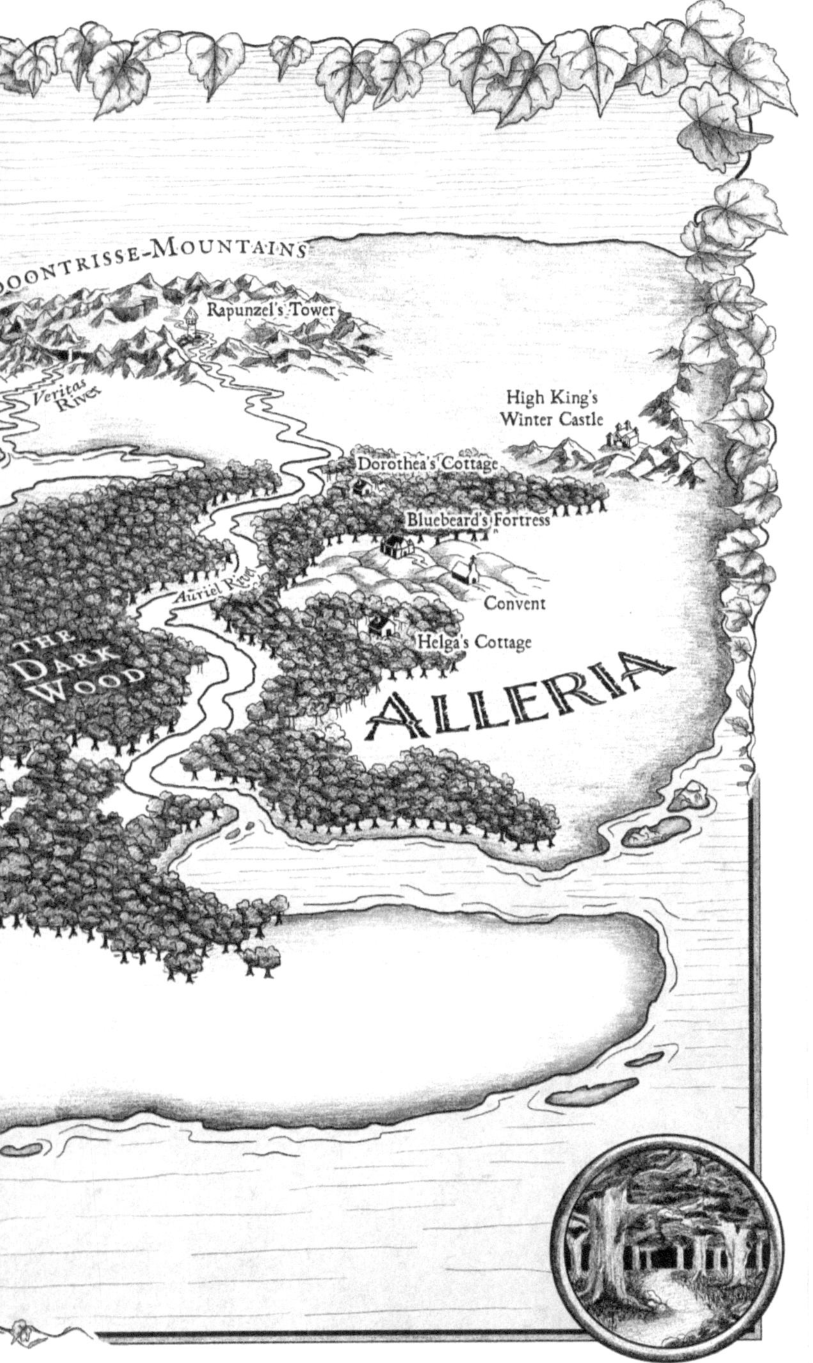
SOONTRISSE-MOUNTAINS
Rapunzel's Tower
Veritas River
High King's
Winter Castle
Dorothea's Cottage
Bluebeard's Fortress
Auriel River
Convent
THE
DARK
WOOD
Helga's Cottage
ALLERIA

CONTENTS

ENCOUNTER

"Watch out, little one!" a kind, burly man calls out in a booming voice when I almost whack my head on a swinging carcass of a goose. He is standing behind a stall where he is selling birds freshly killed. "Wouldn't want you to hurt yourself your first time at market!"

I open my mouth to explain that I am not a novice, though I am a stranger to his village, or kingdom, or city— wherever it is that I am now. I am struck by the bustle of the place I have entered. I could not see anything when I first arrived outside the gate, though perhaps a disem- bodied horse's head and a talking cat would have distracted anyone. I am on the side of a busy street just outside the lowered plank drawbridge of a huge castle. Carts crowd on either side of a narrow roadway heading straight to the market where people huddle and haggle. The odor of sweat mingles with the smells of fresh-baked goods, the season's earliest berries, and lettuce.

A plump woman leans toward the man addressing me.

"She's new here." She jabs a finger in the direction of my baggage and clothing. "Is there something you want?"

I sense resistance in her and realize I must have done something offensive. I shake my head, wishing them a good day. I hurry away while closing my nose to the smells so as not to be further distracted. I follow the main street to the other side of the market square, hoping I will find my way.

As I leave behind both the smells and the sounds of the market, I sense someone following me. I can feel their pacing, the movement right behind me, but each time I begin to turn there is a scurry and the spectre disappears before I have a chance to confront it. I stop and whip around. A young girl in peasant's worn clothing stands before me, her expression too serious for one so young. "Come wiff me." Her eyes are shockingly blue and her teeth still gleam child-white except for a dark hole in the top row where two front teeth are missing. Her tongue flashes in and out as she strives to be understood. "Pleathe, I need you to come wiff me."

"Me?" I feel my forehead bunch at her request.

"Yeth, I have your cat!" The serious expression dissolves, replaced in an instant by an impish grin as she begins to run back down the dirt road, her bronze braids flapping behind her.

Of course, I give chase. Any who can catch Cat is worth being chased!

She scrambles back to the market and I hold my bag awkwardly to my chest. As I run I can't help recalling how I longed to play the game of chase when I was a child. I can almost hear the boys on the other side of the witch's wall as they gave chase to one another. I had always thought what fun it would be to chase and be chased. Listening at the wall was as close as I was allowed to get to people, and when I grew older I was denied even that small contact. The witch imprisoned me in my isolated tower until last summer, when I broke her most sacred rule and allowed a stranger into my life. When she discovered what I had done, she cast me out into this bewildering world of men that she so hates. And the stranger who became my friend and my betrothed? She killed him by throwing him from my tower.

I shake away these thoughts and try to match the child's pace, but her knowledge is more useful than her speed. She darts in and about while I mutter "pardon" and "apologies" as I bump into people and produce alike. I find myself heading between two squatty thatch-roofed buildings farther away from the market and I smack painfully into a wall, bouncing onto my backside.

I look up, dazed and winded. My eyes light to see the troubadour, the "wall" I hit. Here he stands, once more in my life, laughing with the little girl.

"Towd you I'd get her to come."

"So you did, so you did." He smiles at her and kneels to palm her wage. "Now, there's for your trouble."

Her broad grin reveals the open spot in her mouth once more and she nods to me before leaving—"You're quite well, milady?" Just a courtesy; she takes her leave.

"Lady?" I whisper to her receding back.

The troubadour, a friend I made earlier in my travels, offers his hand. I refuse on principle, preferring to pick myself up and collect my feelings of joy at seeing him. Will I never be free of this connection? Do I want to be?

"Are you in truth angry with me, then? I should never have let you leave me."

"You had no choice but to kidnap me."

His mouth slants. "Then I suppose I should have."

I shake my head and glance around, finding the space between the two buildings snug and unusual. Typically shops like these butt up against one another, sharing their outer wall. I hear a rustle. "Where are your friends? Off playing without you?" I notice the troubadour is wearing a brown tunic and leggings, no longer the blue and yellow worn by his small band of renegade entertainers that travel from hearth to hearth. I met them first when I was a scullery maid at a lord's castle; the troupe performed plays while the troubadour wove his lyrical tales into songs. I encountered them in my travels afterward, and though I enjoyed my time with them, there was always something that left me feeling a bit unsettled. Still—I can't deny how happy I am to see him.

"I suppose the players are always at play. We parted ways as friends. I have something I must see done . . ."

I feel myself stare up at him a moment too long and fear I am being taken in. It's hard to look away from those dark brown eyes. "Do you really have my cat?"

"I'd say she has me." Cat comes out from behind him as the length of her black-and-brown tail twines round him.

"No, it would seem she has us." Questions buzz in my ears, but I make them still as I stare back into her luminous green eyes. "What do you want?"

"That dress is close, but won't quite do. Open your

bag; I know Dorothea gave you something better for court."

I comply, not asking how she knows Dorothea, the sweet woman whose home I just left. After all, why shouldn't she know? Nothing else makes sense, why should this?

To my astonishment, all of the lovely dresses in the bag have become rich, ornate clothing for a lady. "Put on your new garments, Rapunzel; you are going to court. You are to be of service to the queen."

I stare at her. "Change . . . here?"

"Yes, here. Turn, troubadour—our girl is a bit modest." She shimmers as she approaches me, stretching out her white paw which transforms into an elegant woman's hand. I cannot speak as the feline/woman comes closer and reaches to touch me. The colors of her calico coat appear in her human form: her hair is jet black, her skin a creamy white, and her dress is tan-brown. I cannot look away from her cat eyes. They remain unchanged in her human face. Something about her feels familiar, but I can't think why. My stillness quiets her and she rests her busy hands for a brief moment. "You didn't think I'd always been a cat, did you?"

The troubadour coughs a bit and the woman resumes her business, dressing me in emerald-green garments I could never afford. She strips me to my chemise, lifts it and gives a slight grunt of approval at the state of my nethersocks. Over my head she pulls a snug cotehardie, embellished with tiny buttons in a line from the low boat neckline to just below my navel. The sleeves stop just below my elbows with long streamers hanging down, which will make it impossible to get any chores done. I know not how I am expected to serve the queen in such attire. In the final layer, she lifts over my head a sideless silk surcoat of light green, embroidered with flowers.

"Your hair looks much better than it did. I'm glad Dorothea was able to fix what that wretched witch did to you." She frowns, referring to how the witch hacked off my hair, the golden braid of rope she once used to climb inside my prison-tower. Cat speaks as she begins refashioning the wimple, putting a flat hat on top and drawing the ends of the wimple over it. "Now, the weather is becoming warmer, you'll appreciate the silk. The Goose Girl, now the High Queen, she caught a chill in her bones some years back when her king got a wandering eye. She keeps the fires blazing even during the heat of full summer. I think she enjoys keeping the fire under him, her small bit of revenge for his finding different mistresses. Of course, he did have to find a woman to give him a male heir."

I simply stare as she straightens me out.

"Poor girl did her best, gave him twelve daughters—"

"Twelve?" I croak.

"Yes, but a king must have an heir."

"And does he?"

"Not yet. First he tried to sire one of his own, but he's given up on that. Now he is trying to find one worthy enough to marry one of his daughters and inherit the kingdom. This is why you will help solve this riddle. Even the many princes who have vied for the hands of the charming girls have failed in solving it. You and the troubadour, however, will find a way." She calms her movements, looking wistful and sad. "That color brings out your eyes.

Go, Rapunzel, you look beautiful. You always have." She vanishes in a wisp and the troubadour turns to escort me to court.

*

My mind feels jumbled, but I try to focus on where I am. It turns out that a court is not at all what I imagined it to be. It is a large hall of sorts with fresh hay covering the floor. There are blazing fires at both ends, roaring with heat. Crowds of people who consider themselves quite extraordinary exchange bits of gossip, I imagine adding and embellishing their own tales. I am still befuddled as I am introduced to the king and queen as the troubadour's ward. I suppose that means we are to be part of the court, but not gentry ourselves.

The royalty is seated behind a large table on a raised platform and I view them from my lower vantage point. They are both dark-skinned like my friend Sister Agnes, so I assume they must come from the Eastern Ports. The fat, sweating king, who rather stinks, bellows that he has heard enough graceless troubadours and has no time to listen to another, when the queen delicately addresses the king, saying she thinks this one might be an exception. Either the king is addled or the queen is clever because he reverses all he has just proclaimed and then asks for more wine, which is sloshed at once into his goblet.

As the troubadour begins to play, singing some tale of the king himself, the queen notices me standing off to the side and beckons me to come close to her right side, away from the king. She is a brittle woman, cold, with thick lips pinched closed. She has a fashionable high forehead, no eyebrows, covered head, and eyes so black I cannot distinguish the pupils. As all her clothing is drenched in dark colors, her entire being reminds me of a dark cloud.

"You are Rapunzel?"

I give a slight nod.

"I see. And do you understand why you have been brought here?"

I shake my head.

"I need you to discover for my husband something. But you must be willing to give the full credit to an undeserving source and let no one know of your cunning." Her fragrant speech is reminds me of Dominico, a friend of mine raised in the Eastern Ports. Her teeth are bright white and her mouth makes a dry smacking sound as she speaks. Her eyes cannot keep to one place; they rove, and I remember to look down as she turns her eyes on me once more. "My husband will soon ask for someone to solve our riddle. You must not accept his offer aloud, but you will solve it nonetheless. All of the fools who have tried thus far have quite lost their heads." Her laugh tells how worn the jest is. "Your troubadour will direct you for the remainder of your stay. Enough, and be gone."

I bow my head and remove myself from her presence, which means I join the listening crowd and wait for the troubadour to finish his detailed song of the king's many exploits. It is long and dull and I smile to think how many other happy-looking aristocrats even now hate him for making them listen. I doubt the troubadour likes his task much.

The meal is served at long tables brought in by a multitude of servants with benches for everyone—except, of course, at the head table, where the king and queen dine on cushioned seats. It is strange to eat with gentry when I am used to serving. We are each given a small bit of many different foods: tender veal pie, blood sausages, yeast bread, strained peas, pears, sugared almonds, chopped-meat soup, and I know not what else. I lose track somehow, but manage to eat just what I need so as not to become too sleepy; the troubadour has mentioned that tonight will be a long night for me.

After the trenchers are emptied and the cups are refilled, the king stands. The entire hall grows silent. "I would only bring a large crowd of nobility here to address a serious concern of mine. My daughters are still under the enchantment of a horrible sorcerer, despite what has been done in the past to rid us of such trouble-makers. None has been found to set our princesses free. For years, each kingdom has sent their best and strongest son, but still, the enchantment lingers. Each morning our daughters wake in their beds with their new slippers worn out, though the door is locked and the windows are barred. Countless princes have accepted the challenge, but not one has kept his head." There is a slight laugh at this. The king sways a little. "Is there no one to free my daughters? Is there not one who can take the challenge and discover within three nights' time what evil has undone my household?"

Worn-out slippers? I am here to figure out why the king is spending all his money on cobblers because his daughters wear out their slippers in the middle of the night? I wish I could rise and leave, but it seems that would not do.

No, I must stay and solve an even greater mystery; why involve me?

Some fool stands up and takes the challenge and is congratulated by the court, and I see the queen looking at me out of the sides of her eyes. The troubadour has a great deal to explain before I go solve this ridiculous riddle.

"What care I for a dozen pairs of slippers?" As soon as we are away from the crowds and heading down an empty hall, I begin questioning the troubadour.

"Not a mere dozen—a dozen every night."

"Fine then, what care I for them?"

He smiles at me as we pass a tall candelabrum. Our movement causes the flames to flicker, and another question enters my mind. If I am his ward, does that mean that they consider me his kin? If so, are we to bed together? I find at this moment that this is a more urgent question, but before I can voice it, he opens the door to a room containing two separate beds. "Tonight you will work, and I, too."

"Who did you tell them I was?" I stare at the beds.

"My charge."

"And how am I to solve this mystery?"

"You will be with the princesses. You see, they have found some way to keep each fool from discovering what occurs each night. They will not expect you to be there. Cat said there is a special cloak in your bag."

I still don't understand to what he is referring, but I open my bag which has been placed at the foot of a bed and begin to rummage through, taking out one beautiful gown after another and placing them on the bed in the sparse room. The very colors of the cotehardies and surcoats breathe life into the drab grays of the stone floor, white-washed walls, and greyed bedding. I take in a breath. "I've never seen anything so beautiful."

"I have." His voice is so quiet, my eyes turn to see a pink hue stain his cheeks before he clears his throat and looks away from me. "There should be a cloak in the bag."

I barely hear him, but I force myself to realize what he has just said. "Oh, yes—" and I stare unseeing into the empty bag. I know that my own cheeks must be scarlet, for I feel them burning. I don't look up until I feel my flush cool. "No, no, there is nothing here."

"Allow me." He moves and pretends to pull something out of the bag. His mimicry of holding a cloak is quite good and I smile and clap my hands together in appreciation.

"The players taught you well."

He shakes his head and begins to drape it over his shoulders. All of a sudden, he has disappeared. I stare like a fool at the spot he was just at when I feel him whisper into my neck, "Rapunzel?"

Stunned, I spin around and whack the air.

"Rapunzel?" Now he is at my left side and I twist to catch him, but instead I fall forward.

I jump up, trying to straighten myself as I look around

sheepishly. "I am not reaching for you again; you might as well take that ridiculous cloak off."

Before me, I feel a stirring. I push against his chest and he reappears as he takes off the cloak.

"Your cloak, my fair one, that you might solve this riddle."

I feel the slow shake of my head as my hands lace themselves behind my back in resolve to no longer touch magic. "You did quite well, just now. You solve the riddle."

"No, I have another occupation." He comes to put the cloak around me.

"What might that be?" I stare at the place where my torso should be.

"A different riddle—and, of course, I have three nights' time."

"Or you'll lose your head?"

His smile is lopsided as he leads me to the chamber in which I must be locked with twelve brats and a brigand. "Something far more valuable."

THE ROOM SEEMS like a gigantic hall. The widest bed I have ever seen stands heaped with extravagantly colored blankets opposite a large fireplace. I surmise that we are right above the queen's fires as I wipe my brow and begin looking for a corner in which to stand.

It is odd when one first becomes invisible, for though you do not realize it, you are quite used to catching glimpses of yourself, various body parts as you move through the day and night. I have kept myself from stumbling, just barely, since first entering the room. I concentrate on not looking at my feet. They know where to go and I try to trust them as when they were visible. I have just navigated safely to the far outer wall when I hear the chamber's door open.

Filing in, oldest to youngest with ladies-in-waiting in tow, each princess has the same pouty expression on the same dark face. Each enters the room with a snicker and readies herself for bed with little need of modesty or decorum. The ladies-in-waiting scramble about picking up discarded cotes, cotehardies, and nethersocks, till at last they bow out of the room. As soon as the door shuts, oldest to youngest, they begin to laugh falling on their shared bed. I can see that their once-dull eyes are now sparkling with mischief.

"Is he like all the others?" One of the middle girls is speaking. Her braided hair is the same black as that of her sisters. It seems as if her nose, also wide like her sisters, should be pinched due to her nasal tone.

"Of course! He will be just the same as the one who lost his head this morn!" This is said by the eldest, I assume, the first I saw enter.

"I almost liked the one a few weeks ago—what was his name?" the one next to the eldest says, beginning to bite her full lips.

"They have names?" the eldest laughs.

"Well, no matter. What we have no one can take from us, and until Father realizes that . . ." and a younger middle daughter slips her finger across her throat.

"Are we quite ready?" The eldest speaks, solemn without warning.

At once, they act angelic and place their new leather slippers at the foot of their bed. They then slide beneath the covers and nod. The eldest, the only one with a sprinkle of black freckles across her walnut brown face, goes and knocks three times on the chamber's door. The door opens wide to reveal the mouse of a man who will soon be headless. I feel a frown on my invisible face as the transformed princess kindly leads him close to me. She provides him with a drink of wine to help him "pass the night as you wait to unweave the horrid spell that has bewitched us all."

She speaks with such conviction, even a tear on her curled black lashes, that I do not wonder that she is the hostess. Once he is tucked in the overstuffed chair, he begins to watch the girls snuggle into their beds, pretending to fall asleep. After a few minutes, he begins to drink with a stupid little smile on his sun-reddened features. There is no question that he would not be the king's first choice for a son-in-law, but after the death of so many princes, one has to accept anyone. I can tell the wine has been drugged, but he is too deluded to realize it. Not even five minutes after he sips the last drop does his head droop and he begins to snore and snort.

"I could never sleep with that noise!" whines the youngest as the girls file out on opposite ends of the grand bed.

"We never have to," smiles the second eldest. "Just hurry and get dressed—they won't wait forever, you know!"

"True enough." I can't tell which of them spoke, and I suppose it matters not. There is such a flurry of skirts and cotes and jewels that I am at a loss until every slippered foot is heading through a door, hidden behind a tapestry. I fall in behind the youngest, making my own feet silent while I try not to touch the girl ahead of me.

☙❧

I THOUGHT to be exhausted by the next morning, but somehow I am not. Indeed, I feel invigorated, as though I had drunk an enchanted potion to keep me alert and alive. I am fluttery as I snap shut my chamber door behind me. The troubadour turns from his tarnished mirror to gaze at me in bewilderment with a razor in one hand.

"Are you unwell?" he asks, as I hurry to hide the cloak and get out a fresh dress for the day.

"Mmm? No, quite fine, though I do not know why. I should need to rest, but I do not."

He turns away from me to finish shaving his face and just above his ears. "Where have you been?"

I don't suppress the giddy giggle. "Where have I not been?" I smile as I pour out his used water from the basin into the chamber pot and pour in a fresh bit to wash my face and hands.

"What were you about?"

I dry off my neck and look around the bedchamber for someplace to conceal myself to change clothing. "What have I not been about?" My skin is still tingling and my stomach feels light.

The troubadour steps forward and touches my arm. "Rapunzel, what is going on? Have you solved the riddle?"

"Most assuredly." I stop for a moment and look into his

eyes. They are concerned, but I can't think why. "I must hurry. The ladies break fast together, do they not? I need to observe the girls some more to understand them better."

"Rapunzel, what happened last night?"

"Magic." I stare harder at him. He doesn't understand and, for now, I don't feel the need to enlighten him. I look away from him and something in me twists, but I will not bend. He is keeping something from me, even more than when we first met. He is too adept at uncovering secrets and I ask myself again why I don't trust him. I cannot. I would have nothing left to bargain with and I would be left empty.

"Rapunzel . . ."

"I need to be alone so that I can ready myself for the morning's meal." I allow myself to look up at him again.

"Of course." He drops his hand from my arm and backs out of the room.

I stand frozen for a moment and then I feel as though I'm falling. I have to catch myself on the foot of the bed for a moment. The rush is exquisite; I cannot fathom what it must be like to taste the deception and joy night after night. I rummage through the contents of the bag and find to my delight another pair of slippers. I place my worn pair inside the invisible cloak and ready myself to join the ladies in the dining hall.

THE MEAL IS BORING, and I think that I and the girls should all fall asleep in our food, but we do not. In fact, I notice they seem far rosier this morning than they did last eve. I myself cannot keep from wiggling and I have to pinch myself to stop.

As I begin to head back to my bedchamber to think through the previous evening, I am redirected to the Queen's sitting room, where I find the troubadour and Her Majesty waiting for me. It is a large hall with tapestries hanging on every wall. The queen is seated in an ornate chair of carved mahogany with her work in her lap. Her graceful brown hands and white palms flash at her needle-point as we speak.

"We have been told you have solved the riddle."

"Yes, Your Majesty." I bow to the ground and look at the hem of her gown beneath which her slippered feet stick out. "I know what happens to their slippers every evening."

"Would you be so kind as to share it with us?" She pauses her craft a moment to motion to me. Her gestures are quite genteel and I have a difficult time imagining that she was once in charge of the king's geese. Hateful crea-tures, geese.

"Every evening they dance them to pieces at an enchanted ball with twelve enchanted princes."

"Where is this enchanted ball? And how do they leave their dedicated escort and locked bedchamber?"

"Well, they drug the poor fool and leave through the hidden door behind the tapestry in their room. Have you never seen it? It leads to a canal beneath the castle where twelve swans wait for them at night to whisk them away to the enchanted ball."

The queen's face darkens as she purses her lips. "But there is only a wall behind that tapestry."

Like an idiot, I open my mouth to retort, "But Your Majesty, I saw—"

The troubadour steps forward and I silence at once. I knew better than to argue with the queen in her own room. "We shall discover what spell is at work here, Your Majesty. We may need more time."

Her round eyes narrow. "You have two more nights." Her nod is slight and we are taken from her presence at once, finding ourselves moved out into a courtyard. We begin walking in the gardens, meandering as we try to decide what to do.

The troubadour looks me over, curiosity evident. "I have a story that might intrigue you, Rapunzel. I have learned a bit more about our queen. Have you heard the legend of the Goose Girl?"

We have wandered into the herb garden, and I reach out, brushing my hands against the fragrant rosemary bush. The grand castle, the High King's seat between Alleria and The Northlands, is situated snugly in the valley between the Midcoast mountains. It enjoys breathtaking beauty no matter where you look. "I have heard a bit; the horse at the gate said something about her."

"The legend of the Goose Girl tells of a princess who traveled from the Eastern Ports to wed and the malicious maid who took her place. The tale goes that the maid kept up the ruse until the true princess, who had become the Goose Girl, was noticed by the king. The true princess, at last, gathered her courage and claimed her rightful place as queen; the maid who supplanted her mistress died, by her own proclamation."

"Why tell me this now?"

"These are the daughters of a match that almost did not happen. Who knows what is at work here?"

As I glance up into his eyes, I feel a wave of confusion engulf me. A bit light-headed, I smile and look away. I have two days, and I must not get distracted.

ENCHANTED

*P*erhaps fatigue has settled in at last after two nights of dancing. Though each night I enjoyed my time of mischief and trailing after the enchanted princesses, I find myself no longer happy. I am back once more with the bratty girls who are re-enacting their same drama from last night and the night before. I am weary and no longer excited about being led once again to a swan, to a ball, and back to the High King's court to unveil this mess (before the slumbering fool who is snoring so loudly I can barely think gets his head lopped off).

Last night I was filled with anticipation. I had little appetite before I rushed out of the troubadour's presence to come and spy once more. All night I danced with abandon by myself, on the outskirts of the ballroom, and I felt I could fly. I will not say I no longer mourn for my beloved, but it is different now. I grieve him in such a way that, though I miss him, I can enjoy the music, enjoy my solitude. I find that I do not hate the witch for his demise as once I did. I still do not like her, nor do I wish to be in her power—but in letting him go, I feel unbound.

But all day long, I began to dread my duty. I knew the night was coming, like death approaching a sick man's bed. I sit here like a stone and I hate what I must do. As lecherous as these girls are, they have found a way to be free from the prison of the court. Not that I think it right so many men have lost their heads for their fun, night after night—but still, have I not been trapped and bound? Must I now trap these brats?

Yes, I must own it. This is my duty, if only to save further slaughter of fools. I rise to follow the youngest, who seems more anxious this eve than before. I should be honest with myself: I do not pity them. I pity myself. I do not wish to leave the enchantment of what tonight will bring. I do not wish to know what will happen next. I will resume my former pattern and move on . . . And the troubadour with all of his secrets? I will leave him behind.

And what of Cat? Yes, another riddle I cannot solve. Too many questions, too few answers. I do not know what I am about, and I almost step off the ledge where we are walking, queuing the swans to gather us on their backs. The youngest whimpers as I tread on her dress by accident. "What was that?"

"What?" Asks the second to youngest, not even turning her head as she steps a dainty foot onto the back of her swan.

"I felt a pull on my dress. I think someone is here."

"Oh, quiet down. Tonight is like all the other nights. Now, come on."

But tonight is unlike every other night. The girls feel it.

Their mirth is forced, their dance hesitant, and I know not how best to catch them, for now, they sense something is wrong.

We enter as always through a clouded door at the end of the canal. I always step through just behind the youngest and manage to follow into their enchantment. Before us are a dozen handsome suitors or apparitions, I know not which. The girls never seem worried about what they are as long as they flirt and dance with them. Each girl is dwarfed by her choice, but happily so. They glide off together in a rainbow of colors in a great hall full of vivid tapestries portraying scenes of great hunts. Their varied skirts sweep the sweet-smelling rushes as they go.

I feel less than nothing, not joy, not sorrow, as though I were a great stone of ice floating downstream during spring's first thaw. I cannot feel. I slump in a corner and wait for it to come to an end.

Until she sees me.

At first, I think this is a trick of the eye, something I am imagining, but the oldest keeps looking my way toward the end of the ball. She watches the corner in which I lurk, and something stirs inside me.

Instead of participating in the next dance, she beckons the second eldest to come and speak with her. They confer and then join their partners, but they seem dangerous, their bodies almost flickering in anger. Their wide, dark faces pucker and their flush drains from their skin. They look nothing like the relaxed and laughing girls from last night. They are strained, and I know what they are planning. I walk with slow steps towards the opening we have always used. I take care and look at myself to know that, yes, I am still invisible. As I near the opening, I hear the music stop and then a scurry of feet. As the opening is still clouded and I have never entered it alone, I close my eyes and pray that I am enchanted enough to get through.

I expect to find a waiting swan before me, but when I open my eyes, I see what appears to have been a woman. Her dark, mottled skin is pock-marked, her face a mass of wounds; her naked, mangled body lies within a strange cage shaped like a massive goose. Her scalp shows through some scraggly black and graying hair, and someone in mercy bandaged her eyes with a clean cloth tied around her head.

"Will you leave me nothing?" she squawks.

I look around me and see nothing but for one swath of light coming from a distant slash in the dark sky. The opening I have come through and the pursuing princesses have vanished. The canal of waiting swans are not to be seen. "Who are you?" I ask in repulsion.

"I am the queen who was before the Goose Girl sought her own."

"Did she do this to you?" My voice is a fragile whisper; can the woman know she scarcely resembles a human being?

"No, I did this to me." Her strange lips pull apart to reveal a broken mouth of shattered teeth. "You doubt my honesty?"

"No, you surprise me."

"I was a mere waiting girl. I saw my chance and dethroned the weak nymph. She became my maid, and then the king's Goose Girl." She gives a strangled laugh. "She would be still, had she not found her strength."

I try to remember the story the troubadour related to me. What had he said happened to the maid who supplanted her mistress and became queen? "I thought you died . . . ?" I halt as I ask. The creature that sits before me would have found death mercy. I touch my nose, trying to cover her stench.

"Certainly, I should have. But I survived my own execution, the death I chose for myself. And I have stayed here, that one day I might have a bit of fun at the queen's expense."

I stare at the miserable creature. How could she, caged away in this labyrinth, have designed the deception I just came from? "And have you?"

"You don't think good little girls are the only ones with fairy godmothers, do you, wench? We wicked ones have them, too. Just ask your witch," she laughs again. It is a throaty, hoarse thing that ends in a cough. I suck in a breath at the thought of the witch's reach into the High King's court. "Of course," she continues, "we are not allowed much freedom once we're caught. Just the ability to inflict a bit of pain on the next generation."

"And have you?" I repeat.

She is silent as she lifts her head, with far more nobility than I had thought possible. She must have been pretty once, graceful and alluring. What sights did her eyes behold that gave her over to such greed? Was her temporary reign worth her present penance? "The Goose Girl suffers, knowing not what has enchanted her girls. The girls will suffer now they will no longer find their enchantment. The king has suffered, never gaining the heir he so longed for. Quite undone, they are. Like me." I suppose the twisted face she makes now is some sort of grin, a grim satisfaction for the havoc she has wrought.

"And of the princes killed?"

"Yes, the witch told me of all the upstarts who had royalty in their blood, but no kingdom to call their own. Second, third, and fourth sons, all. If they had not died on this quest, they would have found death at the lair of some dragon."

She feels no remorse, wants no redemption. "How do I leave you?"

Her head falls forward in resignation, patches of dark scalp visible. Her game is done. "Put one foot in front of the other. Perhaps now I'll die and leave this life."

I close my eyes once more and hear the feet coming from behind me. I climb onto a swan's back and glide away, as though this were part of a dream.

⟡

I'M NOT sure how my feet have taken me here, but I stand in the garden, once more next to the rosemary, and I wait. The air chills just before dawn breaks; the shriek on the wind surrounds me.

"So, what do you think of my little game?" her voice taunts.

"I think it beneath you."

"You don't know what is beneath me because you don't really know what I am about."

I am silent for a moment. Do I wish to be drawn further into her mischief? But I am pulled along and cannot resist for long. "Why should you care?"

"Why should I care what happens in the High King's court? You are not this stupid, Rapunzel! I made sure you had a better mind than that."

"You never educated me on the inner workings of the world of men."

She sighs and the air shimmers: a woman stands before me. It is the witch as I knew her while growing up —her frazzled white hair, her glassy green eyes, her withered mouth, her perfect white teeth. "What do you think? I would allow those who have persecuted us, condemned us to death and hiding to live free without interference?"

"Don't include me in your vitriol—they have not persecuted me."

"Oh, if they but knew who you were, they would not suffer you to live. The Goose Girl Queen would never have consented to have you help."

"Did you want me to help?"

"I have done what I desired here, and now you know how far I can meddle. Your journey has been predetermined, and it will end back with me, my dear Rapunzel. You will see soon that is the way it should be. You will decide I am right."

She is trying to distract me. "What is your true purpose here? Why should you help a servant girl who tried to supplant her mistress?"

The corner of her wrinkled mouth tilts a bit. "My purpose? Do you see now that I have one, a greater one than you ever dreamed? You do see!" She leans forward towards me, clapping her gnarled hands together. "My purpose is the same as it is everywhere I am hard at work.

It is for me to know and you to discover when the time is right."

◦◦◦

"MY MAID?" the queen spits with venom. I am back in her sitting room. She has abandoned her needle and thread and stands next to me in shock.

"She is alive and has sought her revenge," I speak as quickly as I can. I want this done and to take my leave.

"And my girls?"

"They will never find their way back to the ball. They did not find me, though they knew someone had ruined their game."

"Indeed." She takes a steadying breath and touches her fingertips to her lips. An oddly maiden gesture. I wonder what she was like before she set out for this kingdom. Was she never happy again? "And will she hurt me again?"

"I don't believe so. I doubt her powers extend beyond this misadventure."

"I suppose that will have to do." She lifts my chin and looks into my face. "Well, you have solved the riddle. An old fool will marry one of my daughters tonight because of your diligence. But what of you? What would you have?"

"I don't understand."

"Of course you do, child. What prize would you claim?"

I stand there, staring at the queen. There is nothing she has that I desire. I pity her for the life she leads—but of course, it would not do to tell her that. "Nothing, Your Majesty. I am quite well as I am."

"You believe so, don't you? Well, I will have something for you tonight. But first, a token." As she speaks, she gestures for her maidservant to come forward. The woman unclasps a necklace from around the queen's neck and comes to put it around mine. I jerk away without meaning to. "What is it?"

The queen laughs; it isn't a pretty sound. "It is a vial of potion, a love potion. I have another in my chamber, but you may have this one."

"I have no need for such things."

The queen stares at me for a long moment and then nods for the maidservant to finish clasping the necklace. "I say you do."

I nod at the strange queen, and leave her quietly, wandering into her gardens. I hold up the vial to the light of day and stare into its dark green liquid. I tuck the vial beneath my dress and look about me. Spring has had her way here, winding in and out, greening the earth, awakening with white and pink buds those who allowed winter to send them to sleep.

I must be preoccupied to not hear him come up behind me, but all at once, the troubadour is there. I lean over a birdbath, a pedestal which holds a bowl of water with a statue of a maiden wading in it.

"And are you happy?" His voice is low, as though he is measuring something.

I don't turn to face him. I feel mystified as the sun glitters on the water and blinds my eyes. For some reason, I feel irritated. Why was I brought here? What does he have to do with Cat and my witch? What mystery has he been busy solving? What right has he to ask me about happiness? "No, not necessarily happy."

"Really? Most women pretend." I turn to see his playful smile falter.

"I don't need to pretend. When I find happiness, I will know it." I look at him, trying to decide if I should continue talking to him. I can't understand how I feel at this moment. "What of you—are you happy?"

"I think I will be . . ." But he can't hold my gaze. He looks away. "I'll see you at the celebration tonight." I watch him walk away before I continue to stroll down the path.

THE PINK

I think it must have been more cheerful when the fools were beheaded. The daughters seem even more drawn, and it is shocking how hot Her Majesty has made the hall. It would be more comfortable if we were wearing less clothing, but that might be rather embarrassing. I look across the table at the troubadour in misery and see a light smile push his lips to either side. Perhaps he is thinking the same thing about the need for less clothing, so I look away. He is a strange fellow; I feel more heated now than when I first looked at him.

Muddled: this word seems to come to my mind over and over again. In a strange way, I feel sapped of my strength. My mind is bemused, but I am so weary, I can't dwell on the odd mystery I have helped solve. It must be time to move on. Only at Dorothea's did I not find myself feeling this way, with my confusion and tired restlessness prodding me on. Oh, Dorothea, I would have stayed in your enchanted wood forever if you had let me! Of course, as she would say, I would never begin living if I did that.

But as I look around the hall, I wonder—is this living? The queen is married to a man she does not love or respect and so she heats us all. The king is trying to sire an heir by any wench he can find while he marries off his unwanted girls. The princesses, of course, are now looking forward to nothing as I took the one joy out of their lives forever. Though it was an enchanted sort of joy, still they had it. And I? What have I? What is my life now but a roaming from place to place as I strive to understand the meaning of life, its joys, its miseries?

I watch as the eldest is given over to the fool and the king stands to toast them. The king is jubilant during his speech, slurring and floundering his way through it. He then thumps in his cushioned chair with a loud whoosh. And the rest of the kingdom seems thrilled with the end of the mystery. The meal—I now realize a wedding meal—begins to get louder as the ale is passed from hand to hand and great hunks of meat are grabbed. The king stands up again, almost falling, but catches himself and demands music. The music must be from the Eastern Ports, where I have yet to travel. There are large, skin-covered drums that are beaten while dried gourds are shaken to make a rattling sound. I cannot stop my feet from tapping.

Whether or not his company is finished eating, the king is ready to dance. All the tables are moved, the fires cooled, the doors opened, and at once the hall is alive with song. He grabs his queen and forces her to dance with him. Though it is clear that at first she is trying to remain aloof, a slow smile breaks through her stiff countenance. I feel as though I am looking through a porthole, catching a glimpse of the past. I can see the Goose Girl with her curly hair that the prince would gaze at as she watched her flock of geese. Did he know then she should have been his wife? Did he know then how miserable they would make themselves?

For a moment all their troubles are forgotten. At the end of their merry dance, he kisses her full on the mouth and a few knights smirk. "I doubt the queen will remember her promise to me," I say in a whisper, but the troubadour hears me and laughs.

"Indeed, I think she will be sleeping with the king tonight and have other thoughts on her mind."

I feel my face burn and I turn to walk out of the hall, but he catches my arm halfway to my chamber.

"Does it shock you to think he still wants her?"

"No—"

"It shouldn't. A man does not have twelve girls by one woman if he does not want her."

"Then why did he turn to other women?"

"He needs an heir. He was trying to sire a child with others to give her a son."

"To give *her* a son?"

"Of course. He would have the son born, put the wench aside, and give his wife the boy to raise. Otherwise, he would have put the queen away."

My mind races through the implications. How would I feel in the queen's place? How could anyone allow her husband to go into the arms of another?

"Courtly life is not as simple as it seemed in your books, is it?" His voice is hard and I look at him, wondering how I have offended.

"Sir?"

He looks away from me with a slight flush on his cheeks, "Never mind—I'm sorry." He turns and stumbles away.

MY WAKING IS SLOW, a dream just beyond my remembering. What did it mean? I feel certain it did mean something. Colors swirl before my eyes, shapes mesh and I try to reach the dream, try to soak it in that I might understand —but it is gone and I keep my eyes squeezed in tight frustration.

"Rapunzel?" His voice is soft and I dare not open my eyes, as I feel shy once again. I went to bed before he returned, so exhausted I did not even remove my outer dresses or think about the troubadour. Tonight is the first night we are to share the same chamber.

"Rapunzel, are you sleeping? Perhaps I should let you sleep, slip away to do what I must without bothering you further."

I feel frantic. Should I let him know I hear him, or pretend and let his confusion fade away as he leaves? I take a chance and peek open my eyes. "Sir?" I sit up as he places the candle on the stand between our beds near the basin of water. "What is it you must do?"

His intense gaze heats me as he sits on his bed. "Do you wish to know in truth?"

I hesitate. "I believe so."

"Such an honest answer. You do not know what I am going to reveal and you're not sure you wish to know . . .

Rapunzel, I have completed my task and solved my riddle."

"And now you must leave me?"

"Not exactly . . ."

I look at him, his dark eyes mesmerizing. They are full of things I don't know, full of things I'm not sure I want to know. I look away, unsure of my right to ask. "I asked you once of your story—"

"Yes, I told you I had none."

"And now?"

I feel him smile before I look up again into his eyes. "And now I have found it. What makes a man a troubadour? What makes a man a fool? Are these not the very things you have wondered about me? And now, you see, I have been searching for my own story while telling everyone else's."

I feel a shudder course through my body. I know a great truth is to be revealed, and he reaches for his instrument, a lute with a pink rose engraved on it. I adjust the bedclothes to make sure my modesty is preserved while he sings.

"Long ago, in a place better forgotten, a gifted child was stolen while his queen mother nodded off in the garden. Her husband later found her still sleeping among pieces of his heir's blood-soaked garments, and signs of a ravage beast having come and gone. In his rage, the king sent the queen to a tower to die, but angels intervened and brought the lady sustenance throughout her stay. The child, the heir, was not killed but stolen by the king's baker for the child's curious ability to change things through a wish.

"As the years progressed, the child became aware of his abilities and of the baker's abuse. The child's only solace was a girl playmate he grew to love. She was not real, but a wish he once spoke into being. As he grew to be a man, he was determined to find out who he was, what he was meant for. He tried to take his playmate with him, but she told him that she would fade away in the real world. He wished her to become a pink flower he could carry with him, and thus she was carved into his troubadour's lute. As a troubadour, he traveled about the kingdom searching for his story while singing the tales of others. He knew one day he would find it, find the sound of something that sounded true. Something familiar would come to him and he would, at last, know his origins . . ."

His voice hangs in the air and the light of the candle flickers across his tormented features. "You remind me of her, Rapunzel."

"Of whom?"

He smiles and strokes the pink flower. "She could not come with me, but I need you to."

"To what end?" Though I have no direct wish to have the troubadour leave, neither do I know that I should follow.

"I must find my mother and father and set things right. Please, I wish that you would accompany me to my kingdom."

I cannot look away from those dark eyes. What devilry is this? Am I being compelled by his mere wish to join him? But now I know I will go with him. Wherever he wishes, I will not leave his side.

LIBERTY

Through the night we have traveled, a shadow chasing the waning moon. I cannot describe what we were or how we came here, but when dawn breaks and the darkness lifts, here we are.

The terrain is very different from where we were before, and a salty smell assaults me. No longer mountainous, we are near a waterfront of some sort. I can hear the wind pushing and pulling something that slaps and spits and as I look quizzically at the troubadour, he smiles and leads me towards it. His excitement is heightened the further we go and the ground beneath our feet takes on a soft, sandy appearance— not the dark, rich soil I am used to. Then, before us, there is water. Water meets the shore and pulls back into itself. Suddenly, it rushes forward again, white foam bubbling as it reaches to touch the sand and the two collide once more. This is what is making the slapping, spitting sound I had heard. The process begins again as the water pulls back. I feel entranced. I don't know how long I stand here, watching, smelling the air. My steps forward are tentative and I bend low to touch the ground. The sand is gritty, rough between my fingers as I sift it. Awe overwhelms me as I look around.

The waterfront seems vast, but once I look around to get my bearings, I realize that there is a forest nearby and beyond that . . . I cannot say. I can see nothing beyond this stretch of blue, white, and green. I look at the troubadour, who has not moved. His face seems frozen and I wonder at it. Did he not bring us here? Is this not what he wished for?

"What is it, Sir?"

My voice seems to have broken through the melancholy moment. He smiles and looks down at me in—what, adoration? "You should begin calling me by my name."

I stare at him, perplexed. I've never known his name.

"Edmund." He nods at my confusion. "I have learned my name is Edmund."

I nod; what more can I do?

"Well, it is time to find my mother." He begins to walk away from the shore and I follow him, noticing our trail in the sand. We move toward the trees, and though I know he feels we should go there, I loathe leaving the serenity of the waterfront.

"Can we not stay here—Edmund?" I try out his name, but it seems thick on my tongue.

He seems amused at how I have tried to pronounce it, and stops his stride to turn to me. "Rapunzel, we have come to release my mother. Would you have her wait in that tower a moment longer?"

"I'm sorry, no, of course not."

He lowers his head then and touches his lips against mine, but I do not kiss him back. It is the briefest of moments, but I feel everything changed. I am at a loss and I stand here, stiff. He gives me an odd look until the moment passes and then bends again. This time he brushes the back of his knuckles against my cheek and then cradles the back of my head. The sensations are warm and pleasant, but I am still torn as his lips meet mine. Is this what I want? Do I want to be joined to the troubadour in the same way I longed to be joined to my beloved, Paul?

He looks at me once more, part of him disappointed, part of him intrigued. "Time enough for that later," he replies, as though to himself. He takes my hand, lacing his fingers with mine, and leads me into the forest.

I fear it will be a long while before we find anything, for as with many towers, this one has been concealed. But once you know where to look, as the troubadour does, magic no longer hides it. There before us is a grey stone tower. It is reaching far above the trees and high into the sky, the lower half entwined by ivy. Like my own tower, this one is unattached to any other building, with no door, just a lone window.

The troubadour does not hold with ceremony and throws his voice up in the air, speaking in another language. I suppose it must be the language of this island. I have never heard it spoken aloud before and it takes me a moment to understand he is speaking one of my favorite languages to read. "Mother! Mother, it is I, Edmund, your son!"

I see a faint movement and there is a woman gliding towards the window's opening. I cannot see her features, and I wonder what she looks like. I no sooner think this than her son wishes for her to join us and she does.

The good lady blinks and tries to balance herself standing among the bright green ferns that cover the floor of the forest. She is dressed in a pale pink surcoat which covers most of a pearlescent gown, and her white wimple is crowned by a pillbox hat which rests on her head, the tails of the wimple tucked neatly into it. The surcoat is girded by golden chains, whose links are countless and seem to stretch all the way back to the tower, though such a thing should be impossible. The woman is slender, but not malnourished. I suppose this is a credit to the ministering angels of whom the troubadour spoke. Her face is pale and lined, though not drawn, and I would guess her to be in her fifth decade. What startles me most about her face is her eyes—they are dark like her son's, but also very clear, full of something . . . something I would not have thought possible in one so long imprisoned. "Edmund?"

"Mother?"

Though her face is pale after countless years of sitting in a tower, it seems to lose what little color it has, and the poor woman tips forward. Edmund reaches out, catching her as though she weighs no more than a snowflake.

Nearby there is a stream and I use the hem of my surcoat to cool her face with a bit of it. Soon she comes around and stares first at Edmund, and then at myself. "Who are you?"

"Mother, I am your son whom you thought was dead. I have come home to show the king you are to be free." I am slow to translate as I process their conversation, but the emotion is easier to follow.

The woman smiles, tears falling down her cheeks. "My poor son, how I have missed you! Let me look at you." She nudges him back a bit so she can see his form. "You are not a little boy, but a grown man. How wonderful! How amazing!"

"Mother—" Edmund smarts a bit but does not indulge in the emotion of the moment. "Come, you are free!"

The good lady touches her links with a light hand, but says, "I need not you to rescue me, I have been free these five and twenty years."

"But, you were imprisoned because the king thought you killed me," he scowls as he tries to understand her.

"Yes, my body has been imprisoned atop that very tower, but I have been free. The first three years, I fought my confinement. I cried, I howled, I ate little—I could not even see who provisioned me, I was so sure I had been wronged."

"You *have* been wronged!" Edmund is incredulous.

"I have, but you see, I had done wrong as well. Your father had no reason to think well of me." She is slow to sit up and looks at her son with steady, glowing eyes. "I was a burden from the day we wed. I cried and whined at having to leave my father's home for his, I cried and whined when I became pregnant, round and fat, I cried and whined once I had you. I was quite a wretched creature. My melancholy grew worse and I believe that, though I never would have hurt you on purpose, I neglected you, and you could have come to harm while in my care without my trying to stop it. I confess, my son, I cared for myself alone." The dear lady's tears stream down her face, wetting the wimple gathered beneath her chin.

"You did not love me?" Edmund's face is ashen.

"No," she contradicted, "but after three years of hating everyone, I realized at last how much I loathed myself. I saw lined up before me all of my opportunities, since I was a little girl, to distinguish myself. I saw all the opportunities I had to serve others, to serve God. But I confess: I served no one, nothing but my own selfish appetite.

"I cried out, this time in repentance. I begged that if my life were spared, that God would show me in His mercy some way to atone for all the ill I had done."

"What could you do imprisoned?" It is the first time I've spoken, and I have to translate the words before the lady can understand. She looks at me with solemn eyes, feeling, though not yet aware of what connects us.

"I learned to love others, I learned to pray, and I learned to live outside myself."

"How is that possible?" I stumble over the words, but I know they will come more smoothly if I continue practicing this tongue.

"The angels, God's messengers, brought me food each day, and often, visions of things to pray for. It did my heart good to care for others outside of myself . . . And God is merciful, for He started with you first, my son. Oh, how I prayed for you through those first years! It healed me. And then He showed me the peasants who served under your father and his lords, how they suffered for lack of rain—and after months of praying, they received enough to bring in a good crop! He showed me such large things, such detailed things. He changed me. I do wish I had changed before so that none of this might have happened."

Edmund continues to stare at her. "Even my wish would not be granted in the asking of that."

"I know, my child, I know." Her smile is slight and she licks her lips to finish her confession. "My most difficult prayer was the one to forgive your father. I saw how he suffered for his choice, how he had suffered from such a neglectful and selfish wife. All at once one day I went down on my knees and begged forgiveness for doing him wrong, and then I was able to forgive him for the horrible wrong he had done me."

"How can you forgive him?" His fingers glide over the golden links that tie her to the tower.

As she turns her head to look at him without blinking, her eyes see realms and dimensions I could never imagine. "How can I not?" In the troubadour's hands, one link breaks and he wishes us to his father's kingdom.

RECONCILIATION

When we reach the king's court, I am in awe of the queen. She has been ill-used, her life has been unfair—but I watch her face as she sees the place she once took for granted, and I know she has forgiven all that has been done against her. How can I hope to understand such forgiveness? If I can understand it, perhaps I can embrace it as my own . . .

We wait in a dim corridor outside the throne room. The king's audience takes time to receive, but the mother and son seem not to notice it. They are delighted in each other's company; they have so many years of absence to amend. The troubadour relates stories of his travels and, before I realize it, the page is being sent to bring us to His Majesty's presence.

We step into a massive hall, where the stones are the color of the white sand I saw next to the sea. On the far end of the room is a platform on which sits an ornate throne, and on it is the king. The wall behind the throne is covered with a black-and-yellow banner with a large lion who looks as though he'd like to roar. The troubadour steps forward onto a black carpet that leads us to stand before the king and introduces us; he refuses that any other should do the job. "I am your son, Edmund, whom you thought was dead. This lady is the queen, whom you locked up in a tower for my supposed death. This is my beloved, Rapunzel; she has come to aid and wed me." At this, I start and look at the troubadour, but he is in earnest.

The king's face is deeply etched with all of the worries and cares of the past twenty-eight years. His high forehead reveals a dark receded hairline that has begun to grey, uncovered except for a sturdy gold crown embedded with rubies. His stern brown eyes widen and look at us, unblinking. "You claim to be whom? You come to our court to accuse us of what?"

"We come not to accuse, my father, but to redeem the past." I cannot hear the troubadour's whisper of a wish, but all at once I see a large, fat, reddish man suspended in the air before the throne. "Do you recognize this man, my lord?"

The king, still trying to discern what is taking place without appearing the fool, stares into the face before him. "Yes, his name is . . . I can't quite remember, but he does seem familiar."

"He was your baker for a time. His name is Elias. Do you remember

how long ago he was your baker?"

The king appears baffled; after all, he does not handle matters of the household staff himself. "Couldn't say— many years ago."

The troubadour releases the baker with a word. "Elias, I wish you to speak the truth."

Sprawling on the floor before the throne, the driveling fool begins his tale. "Your Majesty, I cannot lie. I stole your child after drugging Queen Lefwenna's meal. On a typical day, the queen napped in the outer gardens and it was simple work to help her along . . ." Here the man falters, his voice compelled forth by the wish, and he spurts out the truth. "I took blood from animals I had butchered and made it appear the child had come to harm. I left soon after, having hidden the babe with my wife in the wood. Your child gave me all that I wished until—"

Edmund breaks in, "Thank you, Elias, I know how I escaped. I leave you in the king's hands now for true justice."

Elias quakes in terror as armed knights are called to haul him away to be held in the dungeon, awaiting the king's pleasure. I can hear his cries even after the massive doors of the court are shut on him. I stare at the king who looks back and forth between his son and his wife.

"So, we have incarcerated our queen for no purpose." He stares at her in challenge.

"No, my lord—you did what you thought was best." I feel like I could choke on this for her, but the queen says it with a clear voice.

He pauses, staring hard at her. "You bear us no ill will?"

She bestows such a benevolent smile, I cannot believe it! "I did. I hated you, but at last I saw why you would think so poorly of me—and for that, for all that I did to destroy your love of me, I am sorry." She bows low to the ground, no pride keeping her from admitting her shame, her pale pink skirts folding in soft ruffles to the black rug before the throne.

The king—I heard him called King Purnell—stands and steps down the few stairs that keep him above the rest. He lifts the lady up; his lips are pressed together, white. His brow is lowered in a grimace. "My lady, far be it from us to not admit when we—when I have been . . . gravely mistaken." He seems to want to say something more, but his coarse voice has stopped and he turns back to go sit on his throne. He nods to Edmund, his brow furrowed, as though in question.

"Sire, I have not heard of another queen or another heir in all this time, but I have thought that perhaps I have not heard the full story."

The king clears his throat and avoids looking at his wife. "Yes . . . no. There has been no new queen, no heir besides you. We had meant to remarry but found we could not. If either of you should wish to rejoin the kingdom of Rona," he hazards a quick glance in the queen's direction, "your places are vacant and need to be filled." He looks down at his hands and collects his former brusque demeanor. "Now, you must leave us and let our servants attend to you. We will see you this evening."

⌘

THE REST of the afternoon I feel pulled and pushed about, as the servants find a place for each of us. Before I am sure what is happening I am standing in my own bedchamber being dressed for supper, though I know not what time it might be. The room is bigger than the one in my tower. There is a grand bed and a window with stained glass of yellow, blue, and red that leave puddles of color on the pale rugs.

As the maid who dressed me is leaving, the queen slips in, her gown trailing behind her. She smiles at me, but I feel nervous in her presence. "My son calls you Rapunzel?"

"Yes, Your Majesty."

She waves a hand as though to dismiss my formality. "Rapunzel—that is a very unusual name. How did your mother come by naming you that?"

"I was never told."

"And you never asked?"

I take a moment to smooth imaginary wrinkles out of my emerald-green surcoat. "No, you see, I was told many stories, and each one led to another until I had all of the truth and the lies my mind could hold, but not the ability to distinguish between the two."

She takes this confusing web of information with a firm nod. "And your mother?"

"She has been lost to me."

"Perhaps that is why my son loves you so. You have that in common. He was bred on lies without his mother as well. I suppose you are a lot alike?"

"I don't know, my lady; he keeps his own counsel."

"But you are to be married."

What can I say to this? I look away from her inquisitive face.

"Forgive me, I want to know everything I can about him—and you are a mystery, but one who holds his heart." She lifts my chin with her gentle finger and smiles into my eyes. "Rapunzel, should we not find the chapel together and pray before we break bread?"

I nod once and she reaches for my hand to lead me.

"I never darkened the door of the chapel except when I knew I had to. Yet, it is the first place I want to visit now that I have returned. You see, I never thought to return, but to live out my days in that tower praying. Now—well, I can scarce believe I am here, and all by my child's doing." She gives a slight laugh. "I must stop referring to him as a child; he is a grown man, about to be married to a beautiful young maid . . . To me, he is still that lost babe I neglected, that beautiful little boy from the first vision I had." Our soft leather shoes make no sound in the stone hall, just the swishing of our skirts as we walk with slow, measured steps.

At the entrance to the chapel, there is a small basin of water where the queen bows deeply and then dips her fingers, making the sign of the cross across her chest. I remember watching the nuns do this in the abbey, but none with as much delight I see on the queen's face. Many were solemn, some dutiful, some serene, and others were joyful. She reminds me of a child receiving a prized gift, perhaps a mere trinket to an adult—ah, but to that child, it is the whole of creation. I smile to see such simple love, and again, long for it myself.

There is no one in the chapel and so we go to the front. I remember all of the things the nuns taught me so that I will not offend her, but none of it must seem natural, for she turns to me and asks in a hushed tone, "Rapunzel, do you believe?"

"I know not of what you speak, Your Majesty."

She smiles up at a large statue of the crucified Christ, though not as moving as the one I admired in the abbey. "Do you believe in our Savior?"

I do not wish to be blasphemous or ignorant, but I cannot lie. "I do not know your Savior."

"I pray you will."

I remember watching Adeliza taking the novice's habit, her soft hands embracing the coarse material for the love of her God who did not save her son from an early death. I give a quiet nod to the queen, but I don't know how to believe, and I don't know that I ever will. I don't know that I want to. How can I explain that though he may be God, I don't know that I trust him to be my God?

I'm not sure any of the three of us knows what to expect when we are summoned to dine with the king. Will we be welcomed with a banquet? Will we be eating alone with him in tense silence or bumbling in our speech to discuss what has happened since the small family was last together? I'm confident only in my uncertainty of how I fit here, though the troubadour and his mother believe I do. The wish seems to compel me to put one foot in front of another and proceed to the dining hall where the king is waiting.

This hall reminds me of the one where the Goose Girl Queen had her meals, but it isn't crowded with tables or a whole court of hungry citizens. Before us is spread a small feast with the king and several of his advisors on another raised platform. As we enter, the king humbles himself by introducing each of us. I notice that he has called in the bishop and a few monks, who are said to be returning from a journey to a nearby monastery where some fellow priests were lacking provisions.

"And are the brothers quite well now, Father?" the queen asks as King Purnell humbles himself by pulling out the seat for her at his right hand.

"They are, Your Majesty. Thank you for your concern."

"Father, I hope that in the future you will allow me to help meet the needs of the people and the Church. They have become . . . important to me during my time away."

The bishop looks at her and nods.

In truth, the queen does not smile more than others, but her joy is evident as she takes her goblet and tastes the wine.

The king clears his throat and addresses us in his gruff voice. "Son, we would like you, your mother, and your future bride to accompany us in three days' time for a ride throughout all of Rona. As you were denied the privilege of becoming a man among your people, we want them to become acquainted with you so that there will be an understanding when you take the throne after our death."

I wonder if it is usual for a newly united family to speak of such dire undertakings right off. The troubadour —I should say, Prince Edmund—nods his head as though this is all well and good. I am still confused about being included, about the fact that everyone seems to think of me as his future bride.

"When harvest time comes, we believe the people will be familiar with you and make glad to celebrate both the harvest and your nuptials." In benevolence, the king now bestows a smile and for the first time looks past the prince at me. I feel I should smile back and so I try, but I think I must be failing, for he looks away with a crease between his dark, bushy brows. "Now, we do not know from what lineage your bride comes, but, given the circumstances of your upbringing and the fact that she has accompanied you from heaven-knows-where to help you back to your proper home, we have concluded that it is God's will you should marry. Her lineage should not be questioned." At this, he gives a shake of his head and stands, his servant moving the chair backwards out of his way on instinct. "Drink! Eat heartily! Our family is home!" He lifts his goblet, and all around the table, people break out in grins and take deep drinks. The king sits again, seated by the fast-thinking man-servant.

I am at a loss—should I be grateful for the king's blessing? But the bishop smiles at me. He is a kind-looking man with his silver tonsure shaved close to his shining scalp and twinkling blue eyes in a sun-weathered face. This is the face and body of a working man, not a scholar. I realize that he has been praying for this boy, this prince since he first sprinkled the babe in holy baptism. In the midst of my confusion and dizzying questions, I feel the need to speak to this man.

I sense a break in speech as everyone eats and I try to smile back at the bishop who continues to look at me. "Father, it has been quite some time since I made my confession. I would speak with you when you have time."

The bishop nods as though he knew all along that this strange girl had a story she needed to share.

*A*s the meal concludes and we are dismissed from the king's presence, the prince guides me out to the gardens behind the kitchen.

"Rapunzel . . ." His voice is low and intimate; it shakes me inside. I clear my throat and step backwards.

"Is this where you were taken?"

He looks around him. In the twilight, he notices the herbs and garden. There are spring vegetables that are being harvested, rows of soft lettuce, peas, and the nearby bushes of berries. He smiles at the freshly planted summer vegetables: rows of beans, tomato plants, the start of squash vines already beginning to meander every which way.

"I suppose it is. I suppose I never thought about it. Why would she spend her time here, instead of inside being waited on by the servants?"

"Because she felt stifled. She was in a place she didn't love, married to a man she didn't love, with a child—"

"She didn't love." He finishes when I break off. "She

wanted to be free, and instead she ended up locked up in a tower."

"There are worse fates . . ."

He looks at me, perhaps seeing me for who I am the first time since he made accompany him by his wish. "What do you mean?"

What *do* I mean? I should shut my mouth before I spill forth more. "Nothing."

"Rapunzel?" He looks at me again, and I wonder if he will compel me to tell the truth. He shouldn't have to. I find that I want to share more with him. Can it be that I want to trust him? Why is there such a hard spot in my heart?

"Being imprisoned was not the worst; losing you, no chance for reconciliation, knowing she had caused your anguish and her husband's pain was the worst."

"But she did have a chance for reconciliation."

I turn from him and bend to brush my hands across the leaves of a mint plant, tearing off a piece to chew on. "She didn't know that. She yielded and repented. She asked for a chance to make amends without ever knowing she would be given that chance. That is her miracle and that is her legacy. You see, you have an extraordinary mother." I rise, fighting the feeling of despair.

He places his hands on my shoulders and turns me to him. "What is your miracle, Rapunzel? What legacy will you leave our children?"

I can't breathe, but I have to speak. "Sir, we have no understanding. We have no children. Why have you told everyone we are to be married?"

"Why have you not contradicted me?"

My mouth opens and shuts; my mind falters. Why haven't I come out and said, "No, we are not to be married"? "I don't know," I whisper at last.

"Do you not want to marry me, have my children? Don't you want to be my queen?"

I give my head a slight shake in the gathering dark. "But I don't know . . . It's—it's too soon."

With his right hand, he gives my cheek a gentle brush. "Too soon? What do you mean?"

"I—" I shudder. I know I have to tell him, but how? "I was to marry another, but he—he died and it is not a year since. I need time."

He withdraws his hand and straightens his back. "Who was he?"

"I don't know—you see, he visited me . . ." Now I feel ridiculous because I am obliged to relate to him all of the intimate details I have held so dear within my heart about our courtship. I tell of how the witch held me captive my entire life and how Paul heard me singing one night. I go on, sharing that he learned to climb my rope of hair into my tower to earn my trust and my love. Finally, my voice lowers as I explain our plan to escape together, how the witch used Cat to discover my secret, and how she punished us—casting me into the world of men and throwing Paul from the tower.

"It was not a proper betrothal," he sighs as I relate the last bit of my love's demise. "It was not even blessed by your father, mother, or a priest."

"Have you not heard me? I had no contact with those people. He was to free me."

"If he wished to free you, why didn't he take you away

the very night you agreed to go? He knew you were in danger even as he left you there for one more night. Rapunzel," he leans toward me again, pulling off my wimple and combing his fingers through my lengthening hair, "I love you, and I would have carried you off that night." He leans down and kisses my lips again. This time I feel something in me, that hard, tight place, begin to yield. When I give him a tentative kiss back, his passion intensifies, full of hunger I cannot understand.

I pull back at once. "I—" my voice breaks.

"I'm sorry. I will give you your year of mourning. By harvest, you will be mine, and you will be glad for it." He smiles as though he has given me a fortune. Perhaps he has, but I cannot reconcile my feelings.

⌖

"MY DAUGHTER, you requested to see me?" The bishop enters with a humble air. I nod to dismiss Plesencia, a maidservant who has been assigned to attend to my every need. The room where I have been waiting is a spacious and airy room boasting of a long window, a fireplace, and several chairs. He stands before me, an emissary of God, and I wonder if he can help me. He is robed in dark brown garb, unusual for a bishop of his position. He looks like a common priest, with his kind but intense gaze. Perhaps those dark, piercing eyes are common to all Ronan men.

"Yes, sir, I need your help."

"I see . . . So you have no confession to make?"

I feel my cheeks warm. "I have plenty to confess, sir—"

"Sir?"

"Ah—I mean, Father—but in the confessing, you will see how I need your help."

The bishop motions to the sitting area in the large chamber. "My daughter, please, sit down; let us begin at the beginning."

That is when I see her; she comes around in front of his robe, her tail encircling him as she comes.

"She cannot begin at the beginning," my cat purrs. "She was not there at the beginning." As she comes towards me, the bishop's mouth gapes open as her transformation takes place. She flows forward, growing into the marble-white woman, dressed in her tan-brown gown, her long black hair shining as it hangs loosely down her back.

"What sorcery stands before us?" The bishop's voice is no longer kind, but full of the authority that can have one burned at the stake.

"You speak the truth, Father, for it is sorcery that transformed me thus." My cat blinks her odd eyes at him. "But one day I shall be done with this enchantment; I know God will set me free."

"How came you by this enchantment? Is this child here an instrument of the Devil?"

"No, she is free of such evil herself and has sought to rid herself of such entanglements. All this, I can attest. But her mother—her mother sold this poor child to a witch, all for a greedy wish. Rapunzel has been the ward of a witch, until the last harvest. It was then she escaped and came to wander the world, looking for truth."

The bishop's eyes now stare hard at me, trying to understand the meaning of it all, and whether or not I deserve to be burned.

Cat no longer looks at him, but reaches for me and caresses my face. "My poor child. I will make amends," she says. And she is gone.

I stand perplexed, wondering if Cat—*is she my mother?*—will return. Can she make amends and free me from the witch?

The bishop blinks once more and teeters as though he is losing his balance. After I reach out to catch him and help him to sit down, he looks around, mesmerized. "I am sorry, my daughter. I know you asked me to come and see you for your confession. Would you like to give it to me here, or would you prefer the chapel?"

I look into his eyes; he seems to have no memory of Cat's confession.

A MISADVENTURE

Our travels around the island of Rona afford us a great deal of time in one another's company. The queen seems to be taking the opportunity to teach me about the graces of becoming noble. I am grateful for her attention, and she is pleased to learn that I know how to read and reason. I have much to learn about station, the Church, and other such things, but I know that by observing her with the king I will learn more than I imagined possible. For the king and queen are newlyweds, beginning their thirty-year marriage anew in the eyes of God and man.

I watch as she watches him. I listen as she listens to him. I observe as she anticipates his needs, his desires. I notice that he bends to her many whims, stopping the carriage often so she can take in the beauty of the outer world. I see how he makes certain her carriage seat is cushioned, her food to her liking. They do all these things without remarking on them. They reach out to one another and learn one another in a new way, a better one, making up for past mistakes. As I smile to think on these things, the queen laughs that they will make new mistakes to balance things out.

Though the carriage is plush, it is evident that the last of the spring rains have left the roads rutted, causing our bodies to collide over and over again. The queen laughs at me when I am jostled into her again.

"Rapunzel, you needn't apologize every time you bump me. These roads are horrible, are they not? If you keep apologizing, we will have no time to have anything else to say." She reaches over to take my hand in hers and squeezes it. I can't help staring into her kind, dark eyes. I can't imagine her as the selfish young woman she claims she was once.

All of a sudden, the carriage jerks to the side and we are thrown sideways with it. I hear the horses whinny in terror, and the carriage jerks again. I hear shouting as I try to straighten myself, but I am crushed by a great many bodies. The carriage is overturned on its side and we are all in a jumbled heap of elbows and knees with a carriage door beneath us and another above our heads.

The pain of bodies crushing me decreases as those on top start to pick themselves up. As we untangle ourselves, the king, who is on top, climbs out the door above us. Once outside, he lays on his belly and reaches down to help pull the queen out as Edmund helps lift her up. Edmund then helps lift me and the king pulls me the rest of the way out. I climb down off the carriage, watching as the drivers are freeing the horses, soothing them with their deep, calming voices. The horses' eyes seem wild to me and I stand as far away from them as I can. The creatures are massive and frighten me not a little.

The trunks that were lashed to the back of the carriage have broken free and our clothes are strewn about, a few things now coated in the muck that must have tripped up the carriage.

I look to the queen and see that she is looking around wide-eyed. The carriage that was following us with our servants barely escaped the same fate. Plesencia and Elizabeth, our servants, have hurried over to us, but the men have run to help with the horses and try to set the carriage right.

The queen is trembling but tries to reassure her maidservant. "I'm fine, Elizabeth. Rapunzel, are you all right, my dear?"

"I don't know what I am," I say in honesty. I feel bruised from head to toe and I know I will be feeling the effects for days to come. We set about gathering the clothes while the men continue the hard work of getting the carriage put right.

It takes some time to get everything situated and by the time we have things righted, we are each of us dirty and quite wet with sweat. One of the axles has broken and a horse has thrown his shoe. It is determined that the driver with the help of two servants will carry the wheel and walk the horse to the next village to employ the help of a blacksmith. The rest of us will make camp here.

I don't mean to think it, but this misadventure suits me just fine. I am not looking forward to the meetings ahead. I prefer the idea of a day outside with no expectations. The days have become longer and the sun will not go down for a good long while. Being near a stream, we go to wash upstream from where the horses are drinking.

As I try to straighten my wimple and hide my hair, the queen gapes at me. "Oh, Rapunzel, I think you have a black eye!"

My eye does seem to be swelling shut and I can't imagine how ludicrous I will look to the lords and ladies we are supposed to be meeting on this trip. I wash my face and tear off a strip of my chemise at the hem to use in cooling my eye. "Well, I suppose I will be quite the sight when you introduce me from now on."

The queen laughs. "I think we all will be quite the sight, my dear!"

Edmund comes over to us and grimaces once he sees my face.

"Does it hurt?"

"Yes, but I suppose it will fade with time."

"A few weeks if you are a quick healer."

"I don't know if I am or not, I have not been hurt or sick very often."

"You've led an ideal life," Queen Lefwenna laughs, but then frowns and touches my cheek. "I'm sorry, I don't know how much it hurts."

I laugh with her; the idea of my ideal life is ridiculous. "It's fine, truly it is. Perhaps Edmund will write it into one of his songs."

The queen looks at her son with interest. "Do you write the songs yourself? I never thought of that. I always supposed they were handed down one troubadour to another."

"Many are. The man who trained me was like a father to me, but I traveled with him one short year before he died. He taught me many songs, but after he died, I had to improvise. I think the first song I wrote was about his death —not a happy thing to sing about."

I think of Paul. Would I be able to ever write a song of his death? The pain of it hits me hard in the chest and for a moment I can't breathe as I envision him plummeting from my tower. I bend down to the stream again and palm the water to my face once more. I don't want anyone to see me cry.

"But some of my best songs are about mishaps," Edmund continues, unaware of my distress. "The Black-Eyed Future Queen may become something I add to my repertoire. I am sure it will become a favorite—" his teasing speech halts and I stand up to look at his bewildered expression. "I suppose that life is behind me now. Whoever heard of a troubadour king?"

It bothers me that he might not continue to sing. I lean in, putting aside my hurt, and I arch a teasing eyebrow over the unharmed eye. "Come now, no one who knows you thinks you must stop. Perhaps you won't sing for your bread, but there are some stories you alone know. Who will tell them if you don't?"

The queen claps her hands together in excitement. "Tonight, my son! Tonight you must sing. I want you to share with us—"

"But I have had no time to prepare."

"You shouldn't need any, should you?"

"I am not used to singing in this language. Elias took me to Alleria where I grew up and traveled around as a troubadour once I freed myself from him. I remember my Ronan tongue from my time with him, but most of my songs are Allerian."

"Then sing to us in Allerian. The king and I know it well. I'm sure he still travels to the Eastern Ports every third year when the High King holds court."

Edmund looks relieved, but I stare at her. "The High King?"

Edmund laughs, "You've just come from his castle in Alleria, Rapunzel. You helped his wife, remember?"

"I knew she was a queen, but he is the High King?"

"And rules all of Alleria, the Eastern Ports, the North-lands, and even my father is subject to him."

"Him?"

The queen can't stop laughing, "I felt much the same way when I first met him and he was still the prince. He was an overbearing oaf of a man when we were young. I gather he is unchanged?" Edmund laughs in answer. "But, our allegiance is to him, and my husband says he managed the kingdoms after the death of his father. His father was a great man." She pauses and tilts her head as she peers at me. "How do you not know these things?"

I look away and Edmund answers for me. "Her guardian kept her ignorant of much in our lands."

The queen nods. "Yes, Rapunzel mentioned something of that the first day we met, but I didn't realize . . ."

Realize what? The depth of my ignorance? Indeed, even I cannot seem to plumb its depths. "I'll go fetch some wood, shall I?" I don't wait to hear whether or not I should, I simply flee by jumping over the stream and heading straight to the trees.

⸙

IT IS LATE when Edmund comes to look for me as the sun is setting to the West. He finds me at the base of a flowering apple tree, twigs dusted with pollen in my lap. "Have you been alone long enough, my love?"

I lift my head to look up at him, but he puts his back against the tree's trunk and sits down next to me. I notice he struggles with positioning his sword. He isn't used to wearing it yet and I worry he will hurt himself—or me!—while he is still learning how to maneuver with it always at his side. He raises his eyebrows a bit. "I didn't expect it to be so damp."

"Is it?" I hadn't noticed, but as I realize the beautiful layers of yellow dress I wear are damp beneath me, I feel it all at once. I huff in frustration and start to rise, but he pulls me back down. "Rapunzel, why are you so upset?"

"I don't belong here."

"In a wood gathering damp kindling? No, I don't suppose you do." He is leaning towards me and moves a curled lock of hair that has escaped my wimple. "You belong by the fire, even if it is smoking. You should already be in fresh clothes, eating well as a princess should."

"I am not a princess, sir."

"I am a prince and not a sir, and I must get used to it. Soon you will be a princess." His lips curve up as though my worries don't concern him at all. I don't know how to feel; should I be comforted, assured, frustrated, angry? I settle for confused. "Come with me. You can add this wood to the fire later, but for now, let's find you something dry to wear."

I allow him to help me straighten and he takes my hand to lead me back to the others.

THE SILENT LADY

Once the axle is mended in the morning, we are able to make our way forward. The first castle we come to is not as grand as the High King's or King Purnell's. It is smaller and made of a dark grey stone that reminds me of the sky just before dawn breaks. Edmund follows his father's example and never lets a servant assist me in getting into or out of the carriage. After the king helps the queen out, the prince reaches for me, making sure I don't wobble off the stool the servants have placed next to the carriage. I see a lord and lady waiting for us, bowing low to His Majesty and Her Majesty and once again to Edmund and I. I catch the quick second glance as they notice my blackened eye.

Three massive dogs bound toward us. I don't even know where they came from. They look to be almost the size of horses, galloping at a terrifying speed. The lord lets out a sharp command to stop, and they halt at once. With lowered heads and their tails drooping, they seek pardon from their master, who pats each head. The dogs then sit next to him, eagerly looking at us.

I take a shaky breath. I hope they don't want to eat us.

"Sir Reginald and Lady Fenella, we thank you for allowing us to come and taste of your hospitality." The king's greeting sounds rather stiff to me, but perhaps this is how he addresses all who are under his rule.

The lady must be the daughter of the lord. The men of Rona, not just men of the cloth, go about with their heads uncovered. Lord Reginald's hair is steel grey with a fringe of bangs peeping over his forehead. Though Lady Fenella's head is covered, her white face is unlined. But he leans in close to her and whispers something after they straighten from their gesture of homage and I realize all at once that they are married. I have never seen a couple with such an age disparity married before and I hope I'm not staring.

"Lady Fenella will be happy to show you to your bedchambers, though I'm afraid she won't be able to tell you much," the lord bows his head and kisses her hand. The lady must be a bit younger than I and seems reserved. With grace, she leads the queen and I inside the castle through a web of dark hallways as the men go off to inspect the armory, the dogs padding after them.

We follow the maidservant as she holds a candelabra dripping beeswax. Queen Lefwenna looks at Lady Fenella with curiosity. "My dear, you are so young, I'm sure you were not born before I went away. The king says you were only lately wed?"

The girl nods. Her huge blue eyes blink once and she looks away.

"I see," says the queen. "It can be a wonderful thing to get married so young. I wish you much joy."

The girl nods again, but this time without meeting the gaze of the queen.

"King Purnell said that Lord Reginald met you in a forest near here a few weeks ago, and you were quite alone."

Again, the silent nodding as we begin climbing an ornate staircase.

"Do you miss your home, your family very much?"

She nods again.

The queen gives a lopsided grin in the awkward lull during which I can hear our footsteps on the stone floor. This castle also does not have anything covering the hard floors and the soft patting of our pointed leather shoes makes a scuffling sound. I wonder what I should say, but the queen seems to find something at last. "Your husband is a good man. If I remember right, he loves the hunt and trains the dogs himself."

The girl—it is difficult to think of her as a woman— looks back at us, at last. She turns her long neck and lifts her chin while her eyes narrow. Bitterness creases between her eyebrows; she looks as though she will speak, but her maidservant turns around and speaks for her: "He does." They bring us to a corridor with three doors, where the maidservant continues, "The prince will be in the east wing, but the rest of you will stay here if that pleases you." She curtsies and opens the doors; the candlelight quivers.

The queen clears her throat as she enters the airy bedchamber. It is evident that it is reserved for noble guests. The windows are long and allow in the afternoon's light which has warmed the room. The four-post bed is high enough off the floor to warrant a step stool on either side to aid the sleeper. There are green velvet curtains tied to the posts and a wood canopy above the bed. Queen Lefwenna is pleased and at once forgets Lady Fenella's silence and simmering anger. Once the queen is settled with her maidservant, I am taken next door. My room appears to be a smaller version of the king and queen's. Plesencia unpacks all of my things and lays out my gown for the evening meal as the others go about their business.

"Lady Rapunzel, would you like me to leave so that you can rest before the meal tonight?" Her soft brown eyes don't make eye contact with me, and the distance this creates is unsettling. I should be grateful to have someone looking out for my needs, but it seems unnecessary.

I nod at Plesencia and she leaves me. I climb up into the stuffed bed and close my eyes, but when I do so, I see the face of Lady Fenella, her lips closed shut, her eyes shadowed with suffering.

⚭

LORD REGINALD IS HOSTING us in his private dining room and I am thankful it is not a grand hall crowded with onlookers. I am not looking forward to the first time I will be seated at a high table overlooking the court.

King Purnell sits in the middle of the table, with Lord Reginald opposite him. On the King's left sits the queen and then myself, while Edmund is on his right hand. Across from the queen is Lady Fenella, still unwilling to look at us. She continues her silence, but no longer seems angry, just sad.

What surprises me most are the dogs ambling about the hall. Are they allowed to roam at will? Perhaps what is more astonishing is that they don't beg, but finally move behind his lordship's chair and wait for his attention.

Lord Reginald leans forward as he addresses Her Majesty. "King Purnell shared with me your mishap yesterday. What an adventure. I hope it does not bode ill for the rest of your tour this summer."

The queen laughs, amusement twinkling in her eyes. "To be outside is an adventure of itself, and as long as I am with my family, I am content."

Lord Reginald shifts as a frown pulls down the corners of his mouth. Perhaps he doesn't like to think of the queen's incarceration. He clears his throat. "Yes, well, when you have good company, I suppose any outing can be a blessing." He clears his throat again and then smiles as the servants begin bringing in the evening's meal. "Ah! The food at last! I think you will enjoy this, Prince Edmund. You see, I was hunting yesterday and we have a great many birds that have come to summer on Lake Sutton just outside the castle walls." He allows a servant to scrape his chair back in order for him to rise as several servants begin to bring in large platters of food. He then begins to serve the meal by loading each of our trenchers himself. I wonder if this is part of the Ronan custom of hosting. He makes sure to toss a few pieces of meat free of bone to each dog who catches it in midair.

"I don't think my wife has forgiven me quite yet, but though they are beautiful, they also make a good meal.

Come, my dear, you wed a hunter, you will have to make do. Even as I dress you in silks, I must also feed you well."

The lady's neck bends low and a single tear falls from her long lashes. She stands and looks as though she wants to say something. Her lips begin to part, but she claps her hand over her mouth and flees the room, leaving us to look after her.

The queen begins to stand. "I think I should go—"

"No, let her alone." The abbot, sitting on the opposite side of Lord Reginald, speaks in an unyielding voice. "She will learn what it is to be a lady in time." I look at the man; he is clothed in silk garments of black and there is a somber look on his pallid face. I can't help thinking that wearing black disagrees with him.

His lordship's shoulders slump forward. "I did not think it would upset her. Perhaps we should leave the rest of the wedge alone."

The queen starts. "I thought this was a goose—you mean this is a swan?"

"I thought they were geese at first. I wouldn't have shot into them had I known otherwise."

"But you sounded as though you were going to continue to hunt them."

"Well, there are so many of them!" the lord begins, but lowers his head at the look on her face. "I'm sorry, Your Majesty, perhaps I have allowed my love of the hunt to carry me too far."

The meal continues in near-silence. I notice we are all picking at our bird as though we've lost our appetites. "It is peculiar that we find it right to eat geese but not swans." Edmund comments.

"Have you ever met a goose? They can be quite ornery!" The queen tries to laugh, but it fails.

"I've met a swan before; they aren't much different when they are nesting or caring for their young."

"But that's as it should be. I like a mother who cares for her young. I wish I had done more to care for Edmund when he was little." The wistful regret on her face hurts me, but it vanishes when Edmund goes to her and kisses her temple. I don't attempt to staunch the smile that stretches across my face at his kindness.

The lord clears his throat yet again. I feel irritated at the sound. "Well, if we can't hunt the birds, perhaps we can take to the forest. Edmund must be a good shot, I'd say."

Edmund looks up, his eyebrows drawn together. "I haven't hunted much and have little talent with a bow and arrow."

"Well, you will when you're with me!" Lord Reginald clears his throat and then laughs. He calls forward each dog by name and starts telling how each breed is an asset in a chase, but I don't understand a word he's saying. He seems jolly once more and it is settled that there will be a great hunt led by the dogs first thing in the morning.

When the ladies rise to leave the men to their discussion, Edmund is the one who moves my chair for me to rise. I whisper to him while the others continue talking. "What's wrong?"

He gives a slight shake to his head. "It's nothing."

"What is?"

"I just—I would like to make my father proud."

I look past Edmund at the king who has said "good

night" to the queen and is now settling himself back into his seat with a full goblet of wine. He keeps glancing at Edmund, his mouth lifting as though to smile despite his stern personality. I think that is as happy as the man ever seems. "I think he is pleased with you."

"But I want him to be proud." There is nothing I can say to this because the queen has reached the door and calls back to me to join her. I give a slight curtsy to the king and go to ready myself for bed.

I found out quite early that the queen is a good rider—or at least was—and will be accompanying the hunt. I, of course, elect to stay behind. I have no desire to make better acquaintance with the baying dogs or massive horses that will carry them to go find whatever they want to point their arrows at.

Despite Edmund's reticence yesterday, I discover that he has put on a happy face and I see him off with a wave. Let them go kill something and get to know one another better. Leave me to the quiet of the castle. Perhaps I should not think it, since everyone has been so kind to me on this trip, but sometimes I think I would rather be on my own once more, trying to find my answers. Trying to understand this world better. I shake my head; these kinds of thoughts are not helpful. Here is a family trying to make me a part of them. Why should I resist? Why do I feel I don't belong?

Plesencia seems a bit shy around me and I can't quite

figure out how to let her serve me. She comes in each morning a bit pale, looking for things to do. She hangs back, as though she is afraid of overstepping her position. I am not used to the idea of someone caring for me, in particular doing things for me that I prefer to do for myself. She finds me getting myself dressed and taking care of my own hair, which I am grateful is growing out again. As I turn to go back inside the castle after seeing the hunting party off, I realize I haven't seen Lady Fenella this morning. At last, something I can send the eager Plesencia to do for me!

"Plesencia, I have not eaten yet this morning. Can you go and see if Lady Fenella would allow me to break fast with her?"

But, of course, as soon as my maidservant is out of sight, I feel silly. Don't I have legs and a voice? Why can't I go find her myself?

I begin wandering around the castle looking into different rooms, poking around, wondering what purpose each room serves. I have never had this freedom to explore a castle before. I have always been a servant, guided and directed by my service. I'm not certain what I think I'll find, though fear lurks in a small nook in my soul as I think of Bluebeard's chamber and his murdered wives. I try to reassure myself that nothing as horrific exists here. Such magic must be behind me.

I don't believe myself, though, and I expect the witch's voice to taunt me as soon as I think this. I hear nothing, there is only silence. Could it be that on this island I have at last escaped her grasp?

My feet have led me into the east wing close to the bedchamber of the lord and lady and I hear something strange coming from behind one of the doors. Perhaps I should knock . . . but I don't. Instead, I gently edge the door open and discover the most absurd-looking room I have ever seen. The stone walls and floors are covered with rugs of green. In the middle of the room, the once-graceful lady is stomping and jumping up and down. Her white-blond hair is free of its wimple and cascading in tangled locks down her back. Though she is not speaking, she is grunting with the exertion. Her white face is pink and her face is damp with perspiration. I can't stop staring when she kneels down, unaware of my observance, and begins to knit together whatever she was stomping. Now I can see that there are knitted garments on the ground beside her. What manner of mischief have I happened upon? Should I say something, or leave her to her strange occupation?

Just as I begin to close the door, though, Plesencia comes up behind me. "There you are!" At last, she has broken through her shy reserve, but this was not when I would like her to become comfortable with me. Her voice is not as quiet as one would like when one is spying on another. "What—?"

Well, there is no point in shutting the door now, so I open it all the way, staring right into the blue eyes of Fenella. "Forgive me. My maid and I were looking for you to ask if you had taken time to eat this morning. I did not see you when the hunting party left, so . . ." My words falter; I can't stop staring at her hands that have paused their knitting. She rises and grabs her wimple, with which she covers the top of her head before leaving the chamber. She closes the door with a loud thud and gestures for us to proceed. I take it to mean that she would like to eat together, or at least she is willing to be polite and do so. I wish I could ask her what she was doing, but once the door is shut behind us, I know that the answers are also.

◌⦿◌

THE REST of the day seems long and I do not enjoy my solitude as I thought I would. Fenella disappears after our meal and I don't dare try to find her or discover what she is about.

Plesencia curtsies to me before speaking, which I find strangely endearing. "If it would please you, might I help you with your hair?"

"My hair?"

"Yes, while the hunting party is gone, I could move back your hairline and pluck—"

I hold up a hand to stop her. "I have no desire to have my hairline adjusted."

Plesencia cocks her head to the side. "Are you certain?"

I gesture to my blackened eye which is still swollen and, I imagine, all wondrous shades of purple. "My eye hurts too much for anything to be done near it."

"Oh, yes, I see. Well, perhaps you could let me arrange your hair for you?"

Is she trying to help me? I have this feeling that her being given to me is to also make me more acceptable. Something in me bristles at that; Edmund thought I was acceptable before we met the king and queen. Another part of me is afraid; I don't think I will ever be acceptable. No amount of manipulating my hairline or plucking my eyebrows will make me so. How can a girl raised by a witch ever find her way into proper society, much less onto a throne? Of course, it would not do to voice any of these concerns, and I find that I have just curtsied back to Plesencia. "Oh!" I stutter, "never mind, do what you must."

But her embarrassed silence gives way to a hushed laugh. For the first time, she looks me in the eye. "Lady Rapunzel, I do not mean to make you uncomfortable. I just wanted to help."

Of course she did. "Yes, well, you will find that I need a great deal of that."

I walk with her back to my chamber where she employs her deft fingers to weave my short, unruly hair into an intricate weave around the crown of my head.

"But isn't this the way that married women wear their hair?"

"Married women do wear their hair up most often, but so do betrothed maids."

"Oh!" Is it right that I wear it this way? I'm still not sure if I am betrothed to Edmund, though everyone thinks that I am. It's odd that though I cover my hair with the wimple again, I feel pretty now that it has been fashioned. I would like to show it to Edmund for some reason and I wonder how much longer it will be before they return from the hunt.

I look over my shoulder at Plesencia. I want to give her something to thank her for her kindness, but what do I have that is mine to share?

IN THE EARLY afternoon the group returns, sweating and jovial. The dogs are proud, or seem so from the way they lift their long noses. By the late evening, the kitchen servants have worked wonders to create a succulent meal to make us forget the poor swan from last night. The returned group is jubilant and the hall is filled with some close friends of the Lord's who went on the hunt. What fills me with joy is how everyone is toasting Edmund with their goblets of wine and hailing him as a mighty hunter. Even the solemn abbot who keeps his tonsure neat and shaved seems a bit less stiff, though one would not dare to call him loose.

At the end of the meal, I have a chance to whisper to Edmund when he pulls out my chair. "Do you see how your worries were unfounded? You are a great hunter! Look at the bounty you brought in!" I gesture to the trenchers full of bones being carried away.

He cannot hold my gaze. He looks away, sheepish.

"What is it?"

He gives a shake to his head. "I'll tell you later."

LADY FENELLA LEADS us into her sitting room where we do exactly that. We sit. Since Lady Fenella does not speak, we drink our wine as the quiet presses in on us. The queen grins as though pleased with the company. Perhaps she does not need the chatter, but I can't quite relax. Something about Edmund's words disquiets me. After a long while, the men have come to retrieve their women. Edmund escorts me out into the garden while the others scatter. He reaches for me, but I pull away when his sheathed sword jabs me.

"This thing! I am always struggling with it!"

I can't help laughing, which seems to ease his frustration. "You used to carry your lute on your back. I'm sure that took getting used to."

"I suppose it did."

"Then, give yourself time. Now, what did you want to tell me?"

He looks away and I wonder what could be so troublesome. "What is it?"

"I wished to be a great hunter."

"I know, I heard you when you told me last night you wanted to make your father proud." I reach for his hand and hold it. It's the first time I've initiated contact, but it feels the right thing to do, I want to make him feel better.

"No, Rapunzel, I didn't just want it. I wished it to happen."

His meaning washes over me, but his distress does not make sense. "Why should that bother you? Haven't you often used your ability to get what you desire?" I can't help the edge to my words, thinking of how easy he must have found it to command me to accompany him on his quest.

"It's not that simple. Each wish takes something from me. I use it when I must have what I want—when there is a greater cost if the wish is unspoken."

"I don't think I understand."

"When I was very young, I didn't understand my power, I didn't grasp what it was I could do. The baker who kidnapped me had me wish for—" But he stops here and his eyes avoid mine. "—Well, what he wanted was never good. I was always exhausted afterward and when the wish was dangerous—"

"Dangerous?"

"Yes, dangerous. Sometimes, when you steal things, people get hurt. I didn't want to use my wishes that way. Even good wishes can be dangerous. It's as though each time I make a wish, I am killing a part of myself. I've learned to live with it, but I promised myself I'd never make a selfish wish again. I'd never make another wish unless it was to see justice done. That is why I wished my mother free and then Elias before the king."

"But then, why make me come with you?" I hold my breath for a moment.

For the first time all evening, his face lightens. "You are mine, and I need you in order to become the man I'm supposed to be. Otherwise, I will give into becoming the kind of man Elias was making me, and there will be no justice."

I nod my head as though I understand, but I don't. There are no words to help me comprehend what he has gone through, or even what he thinks I can save him from becoming.

I FIND it difficult to sleep at night, as my mind keeps wondering whether or not Cat is my mother. If she is my mother, has she been the witch's cat since my birth? What kind of life would that be? Where has she been all this time? And why? Why would the witch make her into a cat? Of what use would a cat be to a witch?

I know enough to know that the witch does nothing without purpose, without reason. I feel certain there is some great mystery to the purpose my mother's transformation serves and I don't believe it is a mere punishment. I turn in the bed and sigh. I hate sighing; it sounds so frail, but I feel helpless in the face of all these questions. I should be feeling free. I'm not even in the same land as the witch anymore. I think I am beyond her—but am I? Cat was here, and she mustn't be free yet. Wouldn't she be transformed if she were?

The questions crowd my mind in such a way that I give up all hope of rest. I rise from my bed and set out once more to wander around. This isn't a good idea—I have never done anything like this within a castle before, but then I've never had such problems sleeping. Perhaps my sleeping was disrupted after my time with Dorothea and the strange dreams that held me captive. Or maybe it was staying up all night and being enchanted with the bratty princesses at the High King's castle.

I feel drawn to walk outside beneath the summer's full moon, so I find my way to the kitchen and slip out into their vegetable garden. Something keeps me moving, though, and I travel on. I am following a path my feet know, though my eyes don't see it. There is a service gate in the castle wall. I find it unnerving that it is unmanned, but I hate the feeling of being enclosed, so I venture outside the safety of its walls.

The moon has cast a silver glow all around me. After descending the castle's hill, I find myself among headstones of the lords and ladies gone before. I feel spooked for a moment, as though this place of rest is dangerous. Silly feeling; those who are dead can't see me, can't hurt me. I squint, but can't make out the names etched in the memorial stones. I reach out as though touching the carved blocks will calm the ominous feeling within me.

Out of the corner of my good eye, I see someone bending over, whimpering while gathering something from the ground.

"Stop it now!" a voice thunders. The trembling girl cries out and drops what she has gathered. Dogs rush forward, yapping, and guards grab her, yanking her to her feet. I see now it is Fenella. The abbot and Lord Reginald motion for her to be brought before them. She is forced to kneel there on the hard ground.

"What are you doing here?" Lord Reginald pleads with her, willing her to speak, as though to prove her innocence.

She says nothing, her head hanging, her hair loose and covering her face.

"You see, your lordship? She cannot speak lies to convince you she is innocent. It is as I have said all along, she has come here to conduct her witchcraft! She must be burned!"

"Please, my love, please tell us why you have come here and why have you been making these shirts out of nettles?" He is holding one of the garments I saw her knitting earlier. "Please, tell me. I know you prefer not to speak, but you must now."

She whimpers again, but shakes her head, still refusing.

"What say you, my lord?" the abbot questions.

"Take her away."

I watch them walk away, but I remain outside, frozen until I know they have all passed and can no longer see me if I move. I find where she was and discover what she was gathering: more nettles. But why? And why wouldn't she tell them what she was about?

WILD SWANS

*M*y maid comes in fussing about as she sits me down and fixes my hair. "What a strange day! Everyone is confused, Lady Rapunzel. Is it true what they say, that the Lady Fenella is, in fact, a witch?"

"I don't know."

"I've never seen a witch before, but I thought they were supposed to be ugly."

"Perhaps some of them are."

"I thought all witches were banished a long time ago."

"That would be news to the witches, I imagine." I try to laugh at that, but fail and so clear my throat, which makes me think of his lordship. "Do you know how the lord is? I have not seen anyone yet this morning."

She tugs a bit too hard on my hair as she weaves. "Sorry about that! The servants were saying he has canceled his appointments for the day. He and the king and the prince were to go riding midmorning to visit around, but he can't leave his bed, so sick is he about her ladyship."

I nod. "Where is she?"

"They took her below."

"Good. Take me there."

Her busy hands stop. "I can't do that, Lady Rapunzel!"

I look straight into Plesencia's eyes; I feel I must do this. "If you cannot, find me someone who can. I must see Lady Fenella this morning as soon as I eat."

❦

As soon as I have finished eating with the queen, a servant appears that I have not met before. "I will take you," she says without ceremony.

"Take you where?" the queen says and wipes her mouth.

"I am going to see Lady Fenella."

"But, my dear, I would not advise that. It might upset the king and his lordship."

This poor, sweet woman, how do I explain this? "Though it is not my intent to upset anyone, I need to see Lady Fenella. Come with me if you like."

"My dear, I do not think it wise. I cannot."

I reach for and squeeze her hand, "I'm sorry, but I must do what I think is right."

I descend two levels following the servant, and as we go downward, the moisture in the air increases. I feel cold deep inside and I shiver, but it feels as though my soul is shaking, rather than my body.

There in the depths of the dungeon, she sits on the

damp, fetid ground, shackled to the walls. I rush to her side, grateful that the nameless servant who led me has brought a candelabra to shine a light in this hole. How could the lord ever send someone he claimed to love into this filth?

Knowledge settles over me, but I'm not sure what to do with it. "You're not a witch, are you?"

She shakes her head. I look at her hands, blistered from the nettles she was gathering. Why would anyone choose to do that, unless there was great love involved?

"But there is an enchantment, isn't there?"

I see the candlelight reflected in the tears gathering in her eyes as she nods.

"Someone you love—someone you love has been enchanted. You want to break the spell don't you?"

She nods.

"How can I help you?"

She is silent, but her tears spill forth.

"Why can't you speak? Why can't you tell me? I need to know how to help you."

She covers her mouth with one wounded hand and I feel as though I am staring into a mirror. No, my voice was not stripped away by the witch, but whom did she allow me to talk to? Whom did she allow me to befriend? I look at this girl, a wife incarcerated by her own husband who believes her to practice dark sorcery. It cannot be true. I know in the depths of my being that something else is at work here if only I can learn the name of it.

"I will find something, some way to free you. Some way to help you."

Her head still hangs low and she no longer looks at me

as I take my leave. I make my way into the room where I found her stomping before. I kneel down where she was making the garments and see there is one that is still there. It is the shirt of a man she was knitting. I shake my head; what on earth would compel her to gather nettles? And what magic could induce her to stomp them and then make them into shirts? I know that if I were to try to knit nettles into a shirt for Edmund, it would not turn out so well. I see there are bloodstains where her poor fingers bled for the work she was about.

As though lost in a dream, I retrace my steps from the evening before. I find my way past the guard now standing at the wall and walk down the hill to weave my way amongst the headstones.

I hear a great flapping of wings overhead. I look up to see a wedge of swans in flight. One of them swoops down and grabs the shirt from my hands. Startled, I let go, but try to snatch it back. I fail. The group flies higher and I run after them in panic. There is something about that shirt—I must not lose sight of it. How could I be so foolish as to loosen my grip? Then part of me laughs at this, for how on earth could I have known a swan would swoop down to grab it from me?

The swans do not fly very high, just over the oak tree-tops that are surrounding the lake. The water is lit as if by fire as the sun's rays are reflected on its surface. As the swans descend to send ripples through the reflection, I have to blink at the brilliance of the sun's light, and when I am able to look again, I blink once more. Am I seeing things? Did the bright light addle my vision? There is a man in the middle of the swans wearing the shirt the swan stole. He begins to swim to shore, the other swans following his lead. I am thankful for the length of the shirt when he reaches land, but I still have to look away from his hairy legs.

"Who are you?" he shouts once he has caught his breath.

I back away from him. "Who am I?"

"Yes, who are you, and what have you done with our sister?"

I look over as five no-longer-graceful swans waddle onto shore. They look a lot like angry geese now and I fear they are going to come over and bite me.

"Your s-sister?" I stammer.

"Yes, our sister whom you stole this shirt from!" He barks while yanking on the shirt and advancing towards me.

I continue to back away, almost tripping as the swans continue to advance. "I did not steal the shirt, I found it when I was trying to find a way to free Lady Fenella."

"Free her? Why? What's happened to her?"

"She was found by the abbot late at night and he thought she was conducting some sort of witchcraft."

"What?!" The swans must be attempting to say the same thing as they begin their noise, a sound that is something between a goose honking and a goat bleating.

"Please, I am trying to help. Who are you? What do you mean asking about your sister?"

"No! I cannot answer questions now! Tell me where she is at once that we may free her!"

I shake my head. "If Lady Fenella is your sister, she is in the castle's dungeon—"

But I have not finished before the man has pulled off the shirt, placing it in his mouth that transforms into a beak. He and the other swans take flight. I run below them all the way to the castle, but they make faster time than I. When I finally ascend the hill to the castle's gate, he has transformed back into a man wearing the long shirt. Now he is arguing with a dumbfounded gatekeeper to let him within the castle's walls.

"Sir," I gasp as I make my way forward through the squeaking-squawking swans, "do you remember me?"

The man can hardly turn his gaze away from the man-who-was-a-swan. "What?" He turns to recognize. "Yes, you are the Lady Rapunzel, visiting with the king."

I nod. "Good. This man needs to be seen by His Majesty the king. And the swans need to be seen as well."

"The swans?"

"Yes."

He looks at me as though I'm daft and I'm certain I sound so. Perhaps I am, but there's no use worrying about that now. "You can't see the king, he'll be with the lord, they are about to burn the witch."

"What?" Now I'm shouting. I try to calm down, I have made the guard warier. "Let me go speak to him—there's been a mistake."

I'm not sure how I've convinced him. The man lets me go inside, but he puts the swan-man under guard and they follow with caution. Once past the portcullis, I discover a large crowd has gathered in the outer bailey. I smell smoke. It is greying the air and I hear a woman's cry. The swan-man breaks free from his guard and pushes people in order to make his way to the foot of the pyre where his sister, the

Lady Fenella, is standing lashed to a stake, with kindling just lit all about her.

"Stop!" he cries, and the swans take flight and fill the air with their noise. "Stop! My sister is no witch, she was trying to free us, her brothers, from our enchantment! Stop, you must stop!"

The abbot shakes his head. "Do not listen to this foolishness! This man will say anything."

Lord Reginald looks old and confused as he stares at the woman he claimed to love, but King Purnell is not so indecisive. "Douse the flames! We will hear what this man has to say before the woman is condemned for all eternity."

"Please, Your Majesty, we are not from here, but from Alleria where my father offended a witch. She transformed us into swans, and my sister alone could save us if she would travel to the woods of Rona and make a shirt for each of us out of nettles." After saying this, he took off his shirt and transformed once more into a swan.

"Set her free!" Lord Reginald gasps, running forward to grab his wife to his chest. "Get her nettles so she can complete the task and set free her brothers. Oh, my dear, no wonder you would never speak!" He strokes her tangled hair as she weeps. "Don't speak now, only free your brothers and then you will be free as well."

My heart twists within me to see him hold her this way. Does he cherish her? He would have stood by and watched her burn simply for what the abbot said. Perhaps even with my time spent in the abbey last winter with Adeliza I will never understand the power of an abbot. Perhaps it is supposed to work this way, but it seems too much power for any man to be able to condemn a girl to her death with so little evidence.

⚬⚬

I WALK AWAY from the castle once more; there is too much fuss about the festivities celebrating our coming and the freeing of Lady Fenella. I need to be away from the barking dogs and the laughter of the Great Hall. The sun is shining bright, but the cold wind chills me as it whines through the branches of the trees surrounding the lake. I stare out as a swan glides across the surface, sending out concentric ripples that will make their way to the shore.

"What are you thinking?" Her voice startles me. I had hoped against hope not to hear it in Rona.

"Are you here, too?" I can't help asking.

"I am where I am needed, doing the work I must do."

"And that includes checking up on me?"

"But of course it does, my daughter."

"I was never your daughter. My mother—my mother is a woman you've condemned to be a cat?"

"I told you a tiger ate her." The air near me shimmers and her form appears, translucent, as though she is here only in part. Her white hair is still frazzled, sticking up in all directions; her back is still hunched, her hands clawlike, her skin wrinkled and puckered around her mouth. She smiles that wretched smile at me and reveals again her perfect pearl-like teeth. "Come now, you should have assumed that any cat I gave to you had a special purpose, just as you have a special purpose."

"Why can't you leave me be?"

"You still aren't happy. You haven't found your place in this world."

"We've discussed this before. You hope I never will and that I'll come back to you."

"I don't hope. I know you will come back and discover what you were meant for all along."

"Meant for by you? You kept me imprisoned all my life —what purpose could that serve?" I throw up my hands, remembering that I wasn't going to allow myself to bicker with her anymore. "I don't need to discuss this with you. Whether I am happy or sad, it is my affair. I will sort through my life and decide what is best for myself. I don't need you."

"In a world where picking nettles can get you burned at the stake, you most assuredly do need me. But enjoy your ignorance for now." Her image fades and all I can see are the bright green leaves behind where her face was staring at me.

⸙

IT SEEMS Lady Fenella cannot stop speaking now that she has knit the last shirt and freed her brothers. The grand hall is opened up and overflowing with well-wishers who are excited by the adventure. The people are talking of the transformed swans and I hear many of them adding details that I don't think are true. But perhaps this is how legends are born. I notice that Edmund has the look of the troubadour about him. I suppose he will be composing this adventure into a song, though I wonder when and where he will feel free to play it. There is dancing and laughing as the evening goes on and I find my foot tapping, but perhaps because we will be leaving on the morrow, Edmund does not ask me to dance. I content myself with watching Lady Fenella and her aged husband. They seem happy, but I wonder if she can trust him.

Our journey settles into a pattern of sorts. Every few days we move on from one castle to another, enjoying the hospitality of the lords and ladies who live under the king's protection on land he and his family have entrusted to them. As we visit, the king invites each family to come and celebrate the wedding of his son. I have grown used to hearing about the upcoming wedding, and I wonder how I should be feeling. Should I anticipate with joy or dread the event that everyone seems convinced will soon take place? My indecisive nature bothers me. Why can't I make up my mind what to do or how to feel?

I often find myself seeking solitude on this journey. The queen excuses herself once a day to pray while the king and prince often take this time to speak with the lord about his lands and the upcoming harvest and various businesses. I search out the nearest garden and try to think.

This is not a bad life; the king and queen are genteel, the prince is kind . . . But part of me wonders why he is kind. Is he kind because he thinks he is getting what he desires? Or is he kind because he loves me? *Does* he love me? Though love may not be an initial ingredient in the marriages I have come across, it does seem vital to have as the marriage proceeds. Respect—this also seems necessary, or else one will dismiss the needs of the other with little or no thought to what they are costing each other. I suppose the question then becomes, do I love the prince, the troubadour, Edmund? No. I care for him, but am I in love with him? No. Could I learn to love him? I don't know. I feel something for him, but is it enough? Do I respect him? I believe so . . . but something about him unsettles me and so I remain unsure.

Thoughts like these comb through my mind as I sit under the shade of whatever tree or bush I can find near the beauty of a lord's garden. It is so important for me to be near beauty now, to smell it, hear it, and be a part of it somehow. I unwrap my head and try not to focus on different times, of what might have been. I've said goodbye to that part of my life and so I turn my mind to what might be.

What sort of husband might Edmund make? Will he be so busy with the affairs of the kingdom that I shall see little of him? Will he be near me always? Will I want him to? If we have children, will he take out his lute and sing them to sleep? If I cannot bear sons, will he put me aside . . . ? My mind attempts to avoid the most obvious, most fearsome question: if things don't go as he wants, will he wish me to do his bidding? His power frightens me, and I desire to guard against it.

THE SEASON WEARS ON, and each castle seems the same after visiting the first half dozen. Though the gardens and courtyards vary where I seek refuge in the afternoons, I can no longer focus on the contrasts and instead, my roaming is aimless. I grow tired of wondering what my purpose is in being here. I know that in time my relationships with the lords and ladies of these lands could prove to be important, but only if I marry Edmund. I cannot make up my mind that I should, but I have decided to try. For the remainder of our travels, I reason, it will hurt nothing to become more devoted to him. Perhaps it has been wrong of me to hold myself away from him. He is trying to be a good man and he thinks that I can help him in his pursuit. What if he is right?

I HAVE SOUGHT refuge again midway through our travels, and I find myself thinking once more of the language of the king and queen, the language of Rona, so different from that of Alleria. I am grateful I learned so many languages from my books, though learning how to actually speak aloud in them has been humorous at times. I enjoy the sound of Ronan words and I am thinking on them as I traipse about the castle's outer courtyard, when I hear the faint sound of a bird calling.

This courtyard is surrounded by spruce hedges and I near them, listening again for the beautiful sound of the bird. Now there are two, serenading, and I long to see them, so I begin to run to the eastern end of the hedge. As I pop through, I see the flicker of silver tails. I am filled with childish awe and I begin to chase them, uncaring of who might see me. I feel all of a sudden as though I could run so fast as to burst into flight myself. As they continue to fly just ahead of me, I run all the faster, my wimple loosening and flapping in the air. They hover and seem to turn to me, then rise higher and disappear, leaving a sparkle behind in the afternoon sky. I gasp for breath and stare baffled into the blue where they had been moments before. I then notice the blue is becoming grey—this cursed island and its daily rains!—so I run again, this time back to the castle, but I am drenched by the time I reach it.

I inadvertently cause quite a sensation at my return, and Plesencia in her eager way takes me to my chambers to bathe me. My mood, now sour through and through, grows worse and I ask her over and again to leave me that I might tend to myself. I try at first to be kind, for I know what it is to be a servant, but I know that my impatience has tightened my voice. At last, my need dawns on her and she takes her leave. I am alone once more.

It is fitting: I am always alone, reaching for something elusive, and failing in misery. I allow myself to wallow a bit while I bathe, rubbing myself without mercy with the brush my maid left behind. I almost wish for a visit from the witch, someone to fight with so that I can battle my disillusionment. Am I not living a dream? Has not a prince chosen me to be his bride? Why then this disappointment?

Why the urge to follow the pair of birds higher and higher? I throw myself back into the tub, creating a satisfying splash. Perhaps tomorrow I will find the birds. Perhaps I will stop trying to escape and find beauty in what I do have.

I ENTER THE GREAT HALL, struck again by its austerity. It reminds me more of the convent's refractory than the hall of a noble-born lord and lady. The walls are unadorned and have only one crest proclaiming the family's colors: purple and white. The benches and tables are few, old and worn. But the lack of prosperity is less troublesome than the atmosphere.

The meals observed in this castle seem different to me. The people are quieter, speaking less often and in muted tones. The Lord Chrysogon and Lady Ahelis are quite proper, but never seem to look at one another or anyone else, always their eyes drifting away from whoever is speaking. Their clothing, though finer than peasants, is quite common. Their halls have very few tapestries, and I have noticed that their trenchers are made of stale crusts, such as I was used to eating from when I was a mere servant. Though they served the obligatory feast in honor of the attending king and queen, the food was plain; it did not last long and seemed . . . Well, sedate. There was no singing or dancing, with two mediocre musicians who played their lutes. My troubadour gave me a scathing report afterward on how he viewed their craft. He was quite funny, but I was disconcerted by the feast itself, the lack of enthusiasm. Was it a sign of disrespect to King Purnell and Queen Lefwenna? A short time ago I would have thought myself to never judge anyone of this rank, but after being in so many castles and fortresses and having lived with many masters and mistresses, I seem to have developed an ability to know when something is not quite right. I see little here to suggest a people who enjoy living. In fact, though there is an element of simple living and a bit of poverty, it seems more than that. I do not feel something ominous here, rather, something odd, something ill-fitting.

I look up from my trencher of leeks and nod my head as Annya rises to join me. She is one of the noble-born who has attached herself to me, an awkward youth now beginning her journey into womanhood. I do not have a moment away from her aside from my afternoon retreats while she and her sisters are at their needlework. Most of the time I find her endearing, but then . . . Tonight I decide to smile at Annya and shake off this deplorable melancholy. There is a beauty to be found, and I will find it even in this bleak place.

The chattering girl tries to interest me in the comings and goings of their small community, how her eldest sister is likely to be married soon and two noble-born sons are vying for her hand. The girl sighs. "I hope when my time comes, there will be one for me." I pat her hand with confidence. Though her family may not have much in the form of wealth, I have met her father. A tall, dark-haired man with sharp eyes, he will marry each of his daughters well, with or without a dowry. He is cunning and devoted to his family. Even during hard times, I have heard the others speak well of how he provides. Annya is a fortunate girl to have him for a guardian and protector. I feel strange and motherly thinking these thoughts and so to divert myself, I lean toward her. "Have you ever seen the silver birds who sing just beyond the courtyard? I have tried to follow them the past two afternoons, I am so entranced by their beautiful song—but of course, I lack the wings!" I laugh but notice the girl just stares at me.

"You've seen the pair?"

"Well," I pause, "not at first. At first, I heard their singing and it was as though they took possession of me. I had to find them. It was such a strange sensation; I had to follow them . . . Is something wrong?"

The girl shakes her head, confounded. "You have seen them? In the outer courtyard, you say? I cannot believe they have finally returned!" Without further words, she runs to the lord and lady and curtsies with difficulty, as she cannot contain her excitement.

"Annya?" The fair-skinned lady's forehead wrinkles in question.

"They have returned!"

A ripple of excitement spreads its waves through the room. "You have seen them?"

"Not I, but Lady Rapunzel. For the past couple of days, she says she has tried to follow them."

"What is this about?" the king leans in to ask the lord, who puts up a straight finger.

"Lady Rapunzel"—Lord Chrysogon looks down the table at me—"is it quite true? Have you seen our silver-tailed pair? Come, stand before us now that we might look into your eyes."

I hesitate to stand, for I know not what to make of these proceedings. Standing in front of the lord of the castle, I feel all eyes scrutinizing me until her ladyship claps her hands together, the first emotion I have witnessed in her. "She has seen the birds! Look into her eyes! They are silver!" A loud noise of assent drowns out the next few words, as I am being pulled to the outer courtyard now to show where I saw the birds. The entire court follows us outside, and feeling ludicrous I try to point out to the lord and lady what I saw and where.

"And they were singing, you say?" Lady Ahelis is biting her lower lip.

"Yes, that is what caught my attention. Truly I have never heard such beauty before in all my days."

The lady catches the hands of her lord and looks into his eyes. "They were singing, my love. They have returned singing!" The crowd now disperses. No one seems to pay any mind to the visitors in their midst; rather they seem to rush about their business as though forgetting the interrupted meal.

The queen, who was seated near me before we were separated in the jumbled exodus, comes to place a hand on my shoulder. "What enchantment lies here?"

The king and Edmund join us, their countenance thoughtful. "It is hard to tell, Mother, when those who might explain leave just as we begin to know what questions to ask. Has there been a rumor of odd happenings in this region, Father?"

"No, I have not heard any such talk. They have always kept to themselves, but we have never had problems with receiving tribute. Of course, the tribute is not great, but they have scarce had a fight or skirmish for which they have asked help for . . . as long as we can remember. Occasionally they send a few problems for me to judge, but never have we had any problems."

"Tell me, my love—what were you doing here?"

Edmund looks at me as though I am part of the puzzle to be pieced together.

I clasp my hands self-consciously and wonder if my eyes have turned silver, as they said. "I often come outdoors when the weather is fine while the queen is at her prayers. I was here yesterday when I first heard a beautiful song, and when I began looking for the singer, I heard another join in. The birds allowed me to chase them, and I confess I did—but then they were gone."

"And you saw them again today?" the queen encourages me to continue as she reaches for my hands.

"Yes. I followed as before, but then they were gone again."

"It does not seem unusual," King Purnell reasons, looking up into the oncoming night. "No, perhaps there is a great deal here that we do not know yet." Queen Lefwenna turns from me to look at him, letting her slow smile fill her face and pink her cheeks. The king embraces her and the two begin to stroll back to the castle, birds and riddles and even betrothed couples forgotten.

As they walk away, Edmund offers his arm and we begin to walk the courtyard together. "Why did you chase the birds?"

I look away from his inquiring eyes. "I am foolish, Your Highness; I felt I needed to catch them—no, not catch them, but—"

"What?"

"It is absurd."

"What is, my dearest?" He stops walking and I turn to him.

"I wanted to fly."

He lifts my face. "Yes, I imagine you did. It sounds like one of my songs, doesn't it?"

I love him like this: thoughtful, poetic, tender. I feel natural with him now, safe. If it could always be like this I think I could marry him. He leans down and gently kisses my lips, but he pushes no further and we glide inside together, leaving the mystery of the birds for the morning.

Darkness gives way to light as dawn breaks before me. Did I sleep last night? I feel rested, but I also feel sure I never closed my eyes, only staring into the heavens watching the bright orb of the moon as though to soak in its entire sublime splendor. I ready myself quickly and bound outside, back to the spruce-edged courtyard, not waiting for Plesencia to help me or anyone to accompany me. Alas, I am not alone, as many others have gathered outside and are gawking at a cloudless blue sky. I think it might be the whole of their gentry, except for one or two and the visiting guests.

Seeing me come outside, Annya runs to me from where her family stands and clutches my hands. "Is it not exciting? To know they have returned, and returned singing! What wondrous news. I believe we are ready for their return. We are ready for anything but to continue to go on without them as we have been doing."

"Annya, I need your help. I don't understand the significance of these birds. Are they some sort of good omen?"

"Omen? You think they are phantoms?"

"I know not what to think, but I see and hear beautiful birds and the whole court is thrilled that they are singing as though they hold the fate of the realm."

The girl is quiet for a time, her lips sucked into her small mouth in concentration. She nods her brown head as though deciding something and then pulls me to follow her. "Come, that you might understand."

I hide a smile at the young girl's dramatic speech. I try to remember myself at her age, but my smile disappears. At her age, the witch banished me to my tower because I had climbed a tree and smiled at a boy. She felt threatened because she was afraid I would escape and leave her behind. As I follow Annya, I see she is taking me to a gravesite in which, I assume, are laid to rest the remains of nobles from generations past. The misadventure with Lady Fenella and her wild swans slows me and my feet stop at the gated entrance. It was not long ago that I trod on similar ground and witnessed a woman nearly be burned to death by what she did at a gravesite.

Annya misunderstands my pause and smiles at me. "You can feel it, can't you? 'Here the peace is heavy, they have given their grief and labors to God; they are done with them now.'" The girl sighs at the end of her speech. "I heard that once. Come—you won't understand until you read the inscription."

I hesitate a moment longer and then remind myself that not every grave need be the site for another misadventure. Whatever these people once were, they are no longer contained by their decaying shells. Nothing here can hurt me. I take a deep breath and stare at the inscription etched into the marble of a rectangular slab sticking straight into the ground. "With singing, they shall return. Helena." I look at Annya after reading aloud. "What does it mean?"

"Helena was our lady's one daughter; she and my lord lost every other child as a stillborn. When she was born, we all rejoiced. Well, no—I didn't. I was not born yet, but afterward, I knew Helena, and I would have rejoiced with everyone else. She was perfect and she loved the birds, and in particular, a rare pair, with silver wings and tail. They say she came outside and sang to them in the afternoons, and they would sing back and harmonize with her."

"Did you hear them?"

"No, but I was never here in the afternoons. My mother likes to keep us busy, remember? Helena was very quiet, don't you see? Everyone loved her, but no one could know her. Not truly. You see, she was a bird."

"What?"

"When she grew ill she cried that she could not be outside, and then when they took her outside she cried because she could not fly away with her birds. She cried when winter came and the birds traveled south, and that is how she died."

Why must all tales contain so much crying? And why does this island seem obsessed with birds? "She died because she caught a chill?"

"No—because she was a bird and should have flown south with them."

This sounds extraordinary, perhaps a bit fantastic. "But how could she fly south? Annya, did she have wings?"

"No! Lady Rapunzel, she was a girl but she should have been born a bird." Annya puffs out a breath of exasperation. "She said they would return singing, and they have! Now things will change. Don't you see it makes us feel as though she herself has returned?"

Still, I feel as though I understand nothing . . . What real significance is this? How can a dying girl's words hold such power over a people? I shake my head, confused. Perhaps Edmund will be able to understand it better than I. After all, it sounds a bit like one of his fanciful songs.

But when I go to find Edmund he is already engrossed with other doings, and it is after our evening meal before I can try to speak to him of Helena's dying words. As we walk outside he is introspective, as though he cannot hear me but is thinking troubling thoughts. We avoid the outer courtyard where many come and wait, hoping to see the birds for themselves. Instead, we walk in the kitchen garden, and though it is not grand by any means, it seems to supply the environment the troubadour needs.

"Rapunzel—" He stops and looks at me, wanting to say something, but is incapable of putting it into words, "Rapunzel . . ." he attempts again, but shakes his head as though resigned.

"Edmund." I have become used to saying his name, though I still think of him as the troubadour. I press on as I place a hand on his arm. "What is it that worries you?"

A crease appears between his brow and he shakes his head once more. "I find I am . . ." He tries to smile at me once more. "It did not used to be so difficult to speak to you, back before I became the prince."

"Perhaps we never had such freedom to speak before. There were so many things we could not say, but now we are free to say whatever we wish, and—" Though this is true, I also remember it being too easy to speak to him at one time. I remember being afraid I would allow him too close, I would allow him to know all my secrets.

"Yes, there are so many things to say. And it is not as easy as it once was." Sitting on the stone wall of a raised plant bed, he takes my hands and looks at me. "Rapunzel. I dreamt my whole life of finding the truth, of finding my family; and now that I have, there is such a great deal of responsibility that it ties me to. I feel restless even as I try to learn the ways of being a king. I sometimes want to return to being a troubadour, singing stories to earn my way, never to disappoint anyone."

"You fear you will fail?"

His eyes dart to my face in the twilight. "Most kings train their entire lives to rule, most kings fight their brothers and often kill them to gain the throne."

"Do they really?"

He laughs. "Well, perhaps that's only in the songs I sing. Still, I—" He stops and looks down.

I feel myself soften and I reach out, sweeping my palm across his cheek and lifting his head up. It feels intimate, but I keep myself from pulling away. "Most men have to fight to find out who they are, regardless of their parentage. Your journey is no different in that. You have found your past, so now you must reconcile it with your future. What do you want?"

He catches my hand and pulls it to his heart. "Would you come with me if I left? If we could return to the road, would you stay with me? Would you leave behind all hope of being queen to be with me?"

My path glimmers before me in my mind's eye—but

still, I cannot make it out. Does my destiny lie with this man? I feel much for him, but I remain unsure. "I don't know. I am not here to become queen, but because you wished me to come."

He seems relieved to hear me utter these words; he pulls me into him and kisses me soundly. I do not struggle against him, but neither do I allow myself to yield. As his kiss deepens, I pull away. "Edmund . . ."

"You will stay with me." He smiles. He seems so sure of himself that I am almost convinced he is right, that I have found my path.

But then the implications of what he is proposing dawn on me. "Edmund, it would break your mother's heart if you left her."

"I know." But he is still smiling into my upturned face.

"Edmund, you cannot desert her, can you?"

"Desert her?" He looks confused for just a moment. "No, of course not—I feel restless, but I think I will manage as long as you are here with me. You are with me."

I feel the full weight of his confidence, "Edmund, I—"

He pulls me into his chest and holds the back of my head with his gentle hand. "Rapunzel, you are everything to me."

I take in a shaky breath—to be everything to someone! I longed to be something, but to be everything! I look away, but he turns my chin. "You and I will have a wonderful life together, one free of strife and free of—" He stops and smiles. "I suppose that only happens in the songs we troubadours sing, yes? And only at the end of those songs, too. After all, without strife . . ."

"There would be no story to tell," I finish, feeling limp.

"So, we will have our problems, but we will have each other." He embraces me, but I find I cannot hold him back. I rest in his arms, feeling empty until I remember what I wanted to speak with him about.

"Edmund," I try again.

"Yes, my love?"

"Well, I think you need to compose a song about these birds. I have learned there is a dead girl involved in this riddle, and I cannot understand what it is all about. Perhaps you might if you try. After all, you learned of the princess in disguise, the dancing slippers. For you, a silver pair will not be much to figure out."

He chuckles. "Your confidence is gratifying, but I believe you discovered the truth in the slipper escapade. And don't forget, you were the one who helped make sure Lady Fenella didn't get burned as a witch. I'm afraid I've been too consumed with learning the ways a kingdom should run to be much help." He sounds weary of that occupation. "Perhaps I could try this instead. We make a fine team, after all."

"I suppose we might . . ." But still I look away from his face.

"It occurs to me that such puzzles might be all over this kingdom, that maybe one day that is all I will inherit, mystery after mystery, story after story—"

"And would that please you?"

"Do you know . . . Yes, I believe it would. I think I would enjoy such a reign."

He speaks the truth, for nothing pleases him more than to uncover hidden things, understanding the story of them, and then putting them into verse. I see stretching out before me a great line of kings, delving into the stories of man, pondering, composing, striving to understand. In solving such mysteries, would not such a dynasty be the wisest this world has seen?

I blink and the vision before me fades. Perhaps my friend Mary shared a bit of her ability to foresee the future with me before I left her and Adeliza behind. Silly thing, that, when it does not seem to aid me a bit in knowing my own path. Ah, well, perhaps tomorrow . . .

SILVER

The morning comes to me, waking me with sweet birdsong. I take my time to open my eyes. I feel whole, rested again, as though every bit of me is satisfied and ready to rise and embrace the coming day. Gone are my somber thoughts. The song lifts me and I seem to soar to the window out of my small bed. I am greeted by the pair when I open the shutters. They are singing on the elm branch just outside my window. My mouth opens and I realize I know the song they are singing. It is a tune I remember from long ago, something the witch would sing when she was happy. It recalls to me time from before the tower, before I climbed trees. It was back before I realized I was a prisoner and still innocently thought of her as a mother. I used to sing it in my tower at night when I wanted to remember that happier time.

My voice lifts, heedless of the wind that is carrying it away to be heard by listening ears. I lean out the window like a child, longing to join my two friends. The longer we sing together, the more certain I am they are my friends. I do not question any of these blissful thoughts; they are more real to me than my physical body. It is possible to join them—if not in flight, then on their branch—and so I climb onto the narrow window and try to reach out. But just as I do, I am yanked backward and I land in a heap upon the prince. My voice shuts up at once, and I see a glimmer of silver before me as the pair fly off. I feel light-headed and don't know why.

Once the prince and I have untangled ourselves, he helps me sit on the edge of my bed. He looks into my eyes with that intense Ronan gaze.

"What do you see, Sire, that concerns you so?"

"I did not notice before, but your eyes are silver now."

"Silver!"

"Yes, they have always been emerald green, but now—"

"How absurd!" I try to look away, but he catches my hands before I can stand up and ask him to leave.

"I became alarmed when your maidservant came to us at midday. She said you waved her away while you sang and sang out the window and never turned your head to see her. She seems a nice girl and I can't imagine you ever being rude, so I thought I had best come and make certain you were quite well."

"Yes, I was singing with the birds. What of it?" I feel flushed to be found in my nightdress with my hair tousled and uncovered.

"Rapunzel, you are not even dressed." He looks at me, his face frowning with concern. "My love, you must be hungry after staying up here half the day."

"Half the day?" My voice sounds very far away and I brush past him to the window to see the sun is high overhead. "But it was just morning when I began singing with the birds. Have I been singing this whole time?" My mouth and throat are dry, and I do feel an ache in my stomach. Perhaps it would be best if I got something to eat. Before the prince has a chance to reply to my nonsense, I push him out of the room and try to shake the discomfort that attempts to hold me. As I don my layers of clothing I stare at the brilliant sky-blue surcoat that delights me with the contrasting rich butter yellow of my cotehardie. I confess, I feel like a bright summer sky! I find myself humming again and the song relaxes me. I continue to hum when entering the hall where everyone is finishing their midday meal. I don't mind the stares I receive from the king or queen or any of the attendants, until Annya comes to stand near me, her dark eyes glazed over in a peculiar fashion. "I've seen them, Lady Rapunzel."

I know to what she is referring, but I am put off by her forwardness, she seems rather irritating this morning—actually, midday. I give her a slight nod.

"Yes, I have seen them, like you. They are beautiful, even more so than Helena used to say! Now we know our land will be quite safe from disaster or famine. The birds are emissaries from God, it has been said. They bestow His special blessing here on earth."

"Is that so?"

"Yes, of course! Have you any doubt?"

I move my head, neither nodding nor shaking it, just wishing the irksome but well-meaning creature to leave.

She should, soon; it is almost time for her lessons for the day.

"I am not to have lessons this afternoon. My mother has spared us that we might go to the special chapel service and thank the Lord for His provision."

Has this God sent the birds to them? If so it seems quite extraordinary to me, though perhaps with all my dealings thus far on my journey it should not. The entire court enters the chapel full of energy I have never felt during a mass before. There is expectancy—no, more than that, a certainty of health and prosperity. As we enter last and are seated at the front of the throng on plain benches, I lean into Edmund as though to shield myself from the spiritual pull that I feel all around me.

This mass seems quite different compared to all the others I have attended. The priest is eloquent as he speaks of blessings promised to the God's people. He shares with a spirit of thanksgiving, but unlike the people who seem to be entranced by the birds themselves, he is entranced by his God to whom he gives credit for having sent the birds. He seems to be redirecting his people back to worshipping the God who created the birds, warning them to not be confused and begin to worship the birds themselves. This priest strikes me as unusual, to say the very least.

It is common for royalty to filter out of a Mass first, and thus be blessed first, while the rest of the gentry and servants wait. When the priest asks us to remain behind with Lord Chrysogom and Lady Ahelis as he extends his blessings to all of the others, I take note of the lift of eyebrows on each face. It is quite a while before the priest is done, but when he returns to the front of the chapel to speak with us, I feel a chill and give a shiver. What might this man of God say to us?

"Our lands are in danger, Your Majesty," he addresses the king without further pomp. "The people here hold a superstition I find most perplexing. Of course, there are many rituals the people still hold from ancient times the Church has allowed them to keep, and neither I nor my brothers consider ourselves above the Church in this or any other matter. However, we thought we had better address the issue of idolatry, here and now." From beneath his priestly robes, he pulls out a silver ornament, a likeness cast of the birds. "One of the brothers found the silversmith making this yesterday morning to be presented as a gift for the chapel. He is hoping to be given an assignment from Your Majesty while you are here to make a much larger one, one that might even rival our crucifix." Our heads turn to look at the beautiful silver crucifix, a shock of grandiose design in the austere castle. "The Church has not recognized these birds as emissaries of God; we should not put them on the same plane as our Savior."

I notice that the lady has begun to weep, tears trailing down her face. She makes no sound, but her husband takes her hand in his and she looks at him in pregnant silence. She nods once, an understanding having been reached.

"If I may?" The lord looks at the king, who nods his assent for him to continue. "The birds are our last remaining link to our daughter, Helena. We would not want to idolize them, as you say, but she promised . . ." His voice wanders off into the silence of unnamed feelings.

"Our faith is a mystical thing, yes, my lord. Though our attachment to Lady Helena and our desire to see the birds is very real, we must not let them distract us from worshipping our true God."

Again I am struck by the directness of this priest; who is he that he can speak with such frankness? I have met quite a few men of the cloth by this time, but this man seems set apart from the rest and I wonder if I should like him for it or not. My own experience with priests, nuns, and monks has left me unprepared for this—this candid manner. I appreciate it and feel I should trust him. There is nothing evasive in his attitude, nothing about him to suggest ulterior motives. This man cares about his people and cares that not one of them be led astray. He speaks to those who rule as one who has a firm grasp on his own authority and will not retreat.

THE NEXT MORNING I rise and find the pair waiting outside my window, hovering as though they learned the trick from hummingbirds. After chirping their greeting, which first alerted me of their presence, the pair is silent and I feel as though they are waiting for something. A whisper of light is beginning at the corner of the horizon, but there is not enough to see by. I have brought the candle over to look them over. Are they spectres? Are they real? I begin to sing, but as they join me, they vanish, and I feel hollow. I know they are gone for certain because in their wake the wind begins to blow. I can hear the witch's cackle. "Did you think they came for you? Magic is so deceptive, one can imagine so much! You think that it is all for you, that you have some secret connection, a destiny unlike anyone else's.

Oh, Rapunzel, you did not think to save this kingdom of their mystery, did you?" She laughs, throaty and hoarse, and I look away in shame. Her ruse worked; I felt special, and now feel certain that I am not. I retreat to my bed, refusing to answer, determined to sleep until Plesencia comes to ready me for the day.

FEARS

e have left the land of the silver birds and have accepted the hospitality of three more lords. They seem quite like all the other lords, a few differences here or there, a different family crest and colors—but other than that, it all smacks of monotony.

I have never spoken of any of the witch's visits to anyone. I did not wish to break the spell or reveal my own gullibility. I cannot help wondering how much of my journey she has controlled and how much of it has been guided by another hand . . . I know not how to rid myself of her, so instead I bury my head in my social duties, though I feel withdrawn and ill-tempered.

Plesencia, bless her, has taken to trying to pull me out of this mood. She found a way at the last castle to make certain to have one of my favorite foods when I break fast each morning. She must have been watching me with more attention than I thought to have discerned how I love sunflower seeds. Of course, the poor girl doesn't realize how they remind me of Paul and the flowers that led him to my tower. Sometimes at night, I'll start to sing; I did it for so long it is a habit. But then I think of how he is gone forever. I can't stop my heart from the anger that wells up inside as I contemplate how my life has been manipulated by the witch. I wonder if she wants me to marry Edmund. Did she have something to do with his peculiar ability to control people with a wish?

It has been a long stretch of road to the southern tip of Rona where we now find ourselves. I have heard the king remark to Edmund how important this particular castle is; the lord handles his affairs quite well and the harbor he employs brings in great revenue for the entire island. "From this one port, ships from all Alleria, the Eastern Ports, even the Northlands come to trade with us."

"But why wouldn't the Northlands use a different harbor?"

"There are two other port cities north of Maer, but they have not the same traffic. Most of the silks are made here in southern Rona, and even those in the Northlands love them and enjoy trading their gems for them."

I look at the king's and queen's jewels, thinking the silk trade must be a very lucrative thing.

Edmund must be thinking something similar. "Is silk all we trade?"

"No, we have several spices particular to Rona that the Eastern Ports just can't seem to grow. They bring us cinnamon and allspice while we give them angelica and juniper. But, I must admit our greatest trade is our Ronan hop. The nobles across the Illyan Sea prefer the ale made from our hop than those made from their own. It has made us quite a bit of money, in particular with the High King."

Having met the man, I can trust this to be true.

"Of course, when we go to High Court every few years, I make certain to bring the king several barrels of ale and he always sets aside casks of wine for me. We will be drinking several on the day you are wed."

I still feel odd when people mention our upcoming nuptials, though part of me seems to flutter at the thought. Edmund does not have many opportunities to kiss me, as his business at each castle is demanding. But the last time he did, something in me gave way, began to yearn a little. I find myself touching the necklace I have worn since the Goose Girl Queen gave it to me. Should I use the vial to help myself love Edmund? I don't want to *make* myself love him. I can't help but compare these feelings to the feelings I had for Paul—will I spend my whole life comparing the two? It is unfair to Edmund, but how can I not? I wish I had someone with who I could discuss these things. There is the queen—no, that wouldn't do. I'm left feeling lost and ungrateful.

We reach the castle at last, but I am distracted by the seagulls filling the air with their caws. They swoop into the rippling surface of the sea and pluck squirming fish. The sound of the portcullis grates on me as it moans and creaks, and at last we are ushered into the inner bailey where the lord and lady of the castle are waiting on us. Their resplendent clothes of bright silks seem garish to me, but perhaps I do not understand the fashion here in southern Rona. Even the servants that care for the trunks and carriages wear the strange combination of turquoise and orange I don't remember ever seeing paired before. Lord Col comes forward and gives a flourish with his hand to the side as he bows low. Lady Horenga, a loud, stout woman of many chins, looks unsteady as she bends her knees to curtsy.

"Your Majesties, welcome! Welcome! We have long awaited this visit and are overjoyed at the reunion of your family!" The man's voice is nasal, but he seems sincere even if dramatic. "Given the hour of your arrival, we would like to invite you to come and eat with us before you bed for the night. Take a moment to freshen up and then we have a feast prepared. You will see the entertainment we have planned for your stay!" The man claps his hands together in delight and I'm reminded of a toddler bouncing on tiptoe in anticipation. The wife, her voice more nasal than her husband's, gives a nervous chortle and a snort comes through her laughter. "Queen Lefwenna, I doubt you remember me, but I have never forgotten when you came to visit my father just before you wed King Purnell."

The Queen is trying to smile, I believe, but there is something perplexed in her expression as she squints a bit. "I'm sorry—it was so very long ago, though I have followed your progress with great interest. I'm so very glad for the success of the port. I know it eased a bit of the suffering years and years ago when food was scarce."

"Oh, my! I did not know you knew of how our trades were going. That scarcity was not long after we were wed. Things were quite bad in Rona, but I am happy to say that when Lord Col bargained for grain instead of our normal trades, that was genius." The woman is flushed with pride.

"Yes, I am certain that his genius is why the king

recommended him to your father to wed all those years ago."

"Well, it was hard on my father to have no sons. Much like ourselves."

"I am sorry to hear that. My son is of great comfort to me."

"Well, the lord has chosen an outside heir, as we have no children at all. I never could bear any, and he refused to take a mistress." Again, she snorts a laugh. "He says I am the best companion for him and he wants no other. We suit each other quite well." She has led us into a corridor in the east wing and smiles. "This is where the women sleep. The men are in the west wing overlooking the sea. They have so much to do and say, we want to keep them near one another so they can make the progress they need to before you have to be off again. I do hope you will be staying for at least a week's time."

"I'm certain it will take at least that long for the men to catch up on all the business of the port." The queen is still unsure about something; she has not her usual way of setting the lady at ease.

"My room is just here if you need anything."

The queen looks at me and her eyes dart away. What is she so uncomfortable about?

Plesencia helps me change into fresh clothing and she reweaves my hair. There is something solemn in her manner, and her cheerful chatter is missing.

"Are you quite well?" I ask, thinking of how considerate she has been of me during our travels.

"Of course, just a bit lonely, you know. Not all of us

have caught the eye of a prince." She is trying to jest, but I hear something in her tone that worries me.

Without further thought, I grab the necklace from around my neck. "I want you to have this." I don't want the temptation near me any longer. I told myself I wouldn't touch magic, and yet I have found myself contemplating doing just that in order to settle my fears about loving Edmund.

The maid looks on me with awe. "What? Are you giving me—?"

"Yes, I want you to have this. I'm told it is a love potion, but as you say, I have no need of such a thing."

"I don't know what to say, I—you have no idea what this means to me!"

"You have been a good and kind servant though I have been ill-tempered for much of this trip. I was going to ask if you could become my lady-in-waiting when we return."

"Oh, I could never be that. I am a maidservant—I'm not of noble heritage."

I give a laugh. "Neither am I."

"I am happy to remain your servant, Lady Rapunzel, but the queen will help you find the right lady-in-waiting."

I know she is right. In my heart I have known I need someone who can help me understand the intricacies of courtly life. I'm sure I spoke with too much haste, but I wanted to do something nice. Still, though, I am glad she will remain with me as my servant.

She looks at me with adoration and slips the necklace over her head and tucks it under her gown with a smile.

THE MEAL IS as extravagant as the clothing, but that is not the grand surprise the lord was excited to share with us. We wait for a troubadour and group of musicians coming to sing the praises of the king or something about the lord. Instead, a jester comes bounding into the room, doing several handsprings and landing with a flip before His Majesty. The man is adorned in the orange and turquoise that make my eyes burn. The man must have springs for legs, because he jumps up and begins to dance over to our table, leaping onto the platform where we dine and then up onto the actual table. He leans over the roasted pig, picks up three plums, and begins to juggle them. He laughs, "Throw me another plum, Your Majesty!" The king does so with a look of concern on his face, but the jester does not pause as he incorporates the plum into his game. Now he addresses Edmund. "And Prince Edmund, would you be so kind?" Edmund chuckles and grabs first one plum and then another, but the jester begins throwing three plums back and forth with Edmund with his right hand while juggling three plums with his left. "Catch," he hollers, and Edmund catches his three, leaving the jester juggling three with both hands. He throws the remaining three to Edmund, who has been putting them all back on the enormous platter holding the pig, and then he does a flip off the table, lands on his feet, and then rolls into a somersault. I think for a moment he is done and I start to clap, but he hops back up and shakes a finger at me. "You must be the mysterious Lady Rapunzel, are you not?"

My throat is dry and I can't speak as everyone turns to stare at me.

"Your fame has been noted, my lady, and we know of

how you captured the heart of the prince. The king is now singing your praises far and wide so that we might all celebrate your upcoming union."

I wish I could fall deep into the ground so no one could see me.

"What we don't know, what we all want to know, is who you are and where you have come from. With your permission?" He inclines his head first to the king and then to the prince. They both nod and an attendant comes forward and moves my chair out from beneath me so that I have to stand. "Come here." He says it with a smile. Having traveled with the players, I know better than to trust this jester's smile. "Eyes of emerald green, face pink and white. Tell us where you've been, show us what is right." He leans close to me and in a low tone that no one else can hear whispers, "I know who you are and I know what you are about, my dear." But how can he? I don't feel as though I do. He smiles again and this time turns to the king. "If I may?"

The king, at last, seems amused. "You may."

The jester picks up my palm and scrutinizes it for a long moment. "The Lady Rapunzel was not raised to be a lady and has spent some good time in the service of others. Some might think this makes her not qualified to be a princess, but as you know, Your Majesty, the king and queen live lives of service for their people. They must juggle"—and with this, he pulls out two turquoise balls from beneath his orange tunic—"the needs of their people with their own lives. They marry to bring joy to the people, they have children"—he adds another ball—"to increase the happiness of the people"—and then another ball

—"and to provide an heir that will care for the people. Everything is done for the people. Lady Rapunzel's life, though it sounds peculiar, has prepared her to become a princess and one day, a queen. She will be what is needed to save her people."

The entire room bursts into applause and as he catches and tucks away the balls, he bows with his own flourish and dances away.

As I return to my seat, I feel my cheeks still hot and I can't stop wondering why the people—my people?—should need saving.

THE POTION

*P*lesencia is worse this morning. She is pale and keeps excusing herself. At last, I must ask her what is wrong.

"Nothing, Lady Rapunzel, I have been struggling much of this trip and I feel quite sick. I wonder if there is something in the food they served last night that doesn't suit me. I seem especially bad this morning. I'm very sorry for—"

But I stop her here. "Please, go lie down and rest. I can take care of myself for the rest of today. Feel better, Plesencia."

She tries to protest, but she isn't well enough to continue very long.

I feel a bit guilty that her departure gives me a sense of release. I take a cleansing breath. When was the last time that I was alone without a maidservant hovering nearby to wait on me? I should enjoy being waited on, but in truth, it is a nuisance to know that every few minutes I will be interrupted by a well-meaning servant for what else she can find to be able to serve me.

⚬⚬⚬

THERE IS NOT much to do in this castle and I find myself roaming about, hoping to avoid the talkative Lady Horenga. Our first morning here, I discovered that breaking fast includes listening to more gossip than I have stomach for. I was encouraged to come embroider with her ladyship and the queen after the meal each morning, but today her ladyship was unwell. Perhaps Plesencia was not the only one to suffer from an irritable stomach. I make my way to the flower garden and accidentally startle the queen who is alone and sitting on the ground. She looks up at me, as though I have caught her at something.

"Your Majesty, I missed you at the meal this morning."

She looks away and touches the petals of a red rose. "Yes, I know. I should have joined you. I'm sorry."

"Lady Horenga and my maid were unwell this morning, I thought perhaps you were, too?"

She is quiet. The slump of her shoulders seems strange to me. "I am, but not in the way you think."

"Would you like me to leave you?"

"Rapunzel . . . Come and sit with me, if you would."

The heady scent of roses fills the air as she plucks the petals and lets them fall to her lap. "Rapunzel," she takes a shaky breath, "I never wanted to come here. Of all the places we visited in our early marriage, I embarrassed myself here more than anywhere else."

"But that's in the past, Your Majesty."

"It doesn't feel like it is past—I remember it as though it were yesterday. I was a spiteful harpy to the king. I said things, I did things to push him away."

"You've said as much to me before. I thought you were forgiven."

Her fingers continue to strip the bush of its blooms and her lap is covered in the blood-red petals now. "It has been a long time since I thought of the things I said and did here. I know in my mind that I am forgiven, but if His Majesty remembers as I do what I said the last night we were here—I just don't see how he can love me.

"No matter where I go in this castle, I cannot escape the smell of fish. It always makes me think of it."

I tilt my head to the side, "I can't see anything of the young woman you said you once were. You are kind, generous, and humble. You are loving and beautiful. Perhaps you were selfish and did something horrible, but you were forgiven and he has made you his wife again. I see nothing in his manner that suggests he still holds anger from the past."

A tear falls from her lashes. "Oh, sweet Rapunzel! How I needed to hear these words."

"I know very little of the world we live in, Your Majesty, but I do know you are loved."

The queen reaches over and grasps my hand, "I am grateful God has placed you in my life. You are a treasure, my dear." She breathes in deeply and wipes her face free of tears. "Now, I believe I will need your help getting up."

I laugh. "Of course! It would be my honor."

Except for my exchange with the queen, the day is uneventful until the evening when we all come to dine together in the Great Hall once more. The foods they serve are dominated by saltwater creatures from the Illyan Sea, things I have never tasted before. There is eel, crab, shrimp, and lobster. I didn't touch any of these unusual meats last evening, since I was so tired I felt queasy, but I want to be a bit more adventurous now. I wonder what it will be like, taste like. As the tender flesh of a crab enters my mouth, I am intoxicated by the salty rich broth that it must have been cooked in. I am glad the attendants take care to pull the flesh from the shells for the women; Edmund looks as though he is struggling with his.

As I continue to chew, I see the queen is nibbling. I try not to laugh, for she must hate the food! I've never seen her with such an expression before. She is kind and finds something good in every situation, but this is beyond her. The king sees her predicament as well and recommends something to an attendant who takes her trencher away and replaces it with cooked fruit and bread. Queen Lefwenna beams at her husband and he toasts her with his upraised goblet.

This short exchange warms me and I look over at Edmund. He has said we will grow to love one another. Could it be possible? Will we look after one another the way the king and queen do? I'm afraid that I find his moodiness frustrating and I don't want to be around him when he is like that. Is that something that married people must suffer through? It seems likely that if I chose to marry, there will be times that I am annoyed. Inside myself, I laugh at the thought, for I'm sure I myself am annoying at times. Poor husband—whether he is Edmund or someone else, I will not be an ideal wife.

Just as was the case the previous evening, the jester bursts through the huge oak doors and handsprings and flips his way before us. He does not elect to juggle this evening but instead takes in hand the lute he has set on the end of our table. He walks over to Edmund and laughs. "Poor troubadour prince, I can see you still love to sing your songs, would you care to—?" He holds out the lute, like an offering, but Edmund gestures to the food he has before him and stuffs a huge bite in his mouth, causing everyone to laugh.

"I see, so I will have to pick the song." The jester strums the chords. "There is a song that has been caught in my mind and I pray you will indulge me by listening to the beginning and waiting till the end before you judge if it is a good tale or no." He begins to strum and then tap the lute in rhythm. The melody transports us so that we can see the scene he describes. For the first time since I met Edmund, I do not judge the voice of the singer, I only listen to the tale. I feel as though I have been bewitched.

His voice is higher than I expected and he tells of a storm so wild that no person would want to be caught in it. The pounding at the gate of the castle raises the alarm. The gatekeeper sees the fragile form of the waif waiting there, drenched in the downpour. He takes her inside the gatehouse, where, just as he is about to invite her to come where his wife can care for her, there is another pounding. Here the jester strikes his lute again as though he is knocking on the door. The young prince is at the gate, he continues, just returned from court where he could not find a bride for his liking. Again. The jester waggles his eyebrows at this and we laugh. The young man sees the waif who is trembling with cold and he asks who she is. So weak from fatigue, the girl pitches forward in a faint, but the prince grabs her and carries her into the castle.

The following day, she dines with the king and queen and their picky son. He can't look away from her face, for there is something there that has captured him. His mother is picky, too, and she does not trust the girl who claims she is a princess. A princess of what? She can't say—she has had to run away for her own safety. Again, the jester waggles those dark bushy brows, adding a pause in the music so that we can laugh. Like a good mother, she decides to test the waif, who seems too tired to hold her head up and faints anytime anyone questions her lineage. From the kitchen, the queen procures a hard, dry pea. It is tiny, and she has it placed under ten mattresses filled with the softest down. With murmurs of well-wishes for great rest, the queen sends the waif off to sleep, to rest and recover from her trials.

The next morning the waif is a fright—she is bruised all over! The jester's eyebrows shoot up into his fringed bangs. The waif complains she could not rest because every which way she lay, she hurt and ached. Her delicate nature proves her to be the princess she claimed. The queen confesses her little trick and the prince is told he may marry the girl. All is well in the end.

The jester finishes plucking out the last strands of the melody, but instead of leaving the room, he looks at me. "Should we put a pea under your downy mattress, Lady Rapunzel?"

"As you have said, I have been a servant, and if you were to place one pea or one thousand, you might find me snoring. You would discover that I am no princess."

"Yet," Edmund says with authority.

"Yet," echoes the king.

The queen raises her goblet, and if she had eyebrows, they would be raised as well. She finishes the last of her bread.

The jester grins and bows. "Lady Rapunzel, you will make a king very happy indeed!" And after he puts back his lute, he flips and handsprings away.

◈

"STRANGE MAN, THAT JESTER," Edmund remarks to me later as he walks me to my room. Though the custom often has us women leave the men to talk, this lord likes to have us all together until bedtime. By the end of the evening, it is so loud that my head aches, but I don't wish to seem rude by leaving too early. "How do you mean?"

"Well, as you are aware, I've known all sorts of entertainers."

"I believe you have."

"But he seems very sure of himself, as though he knows things, as though he is telling us something."

"To be honest, apart from the jumping and juggling, he reminds me quite a lot of you."

Edmund shuffles back a step. "Me?"

"Yes, he sounds like he knows things, but he is also trying to find out more answers. Perhaps he's your brother."

"I don't have a brother."

"You could."

"No, I couldn't."

"Well, perhaps not—but still, he could be your brother." I give a merry laugh as he gives a mock frown. All at once he kisses me. It's been a while since we have been alone and he has had the chance to kiss me. It surprises me, but if we are to be married, perhaps it shouldn't. Still . . ."What was that for?"

"Because I love you and I long to make you mine."

"I thought you said I was yours."

"Most of you is—and very soon you will be completely mine." He is so sure of himself and of me. As he leans in to kiss me again, I move away.

"Sometimes, I feel as though I am the tune you are playing, the song you are singing."

"That's as it should be." He smiles and this time I don't move away from his kiss.

"Should it?"

"I am to be your husband—it is only right." He seems pleased as he opens my door so that I may enter.

THE NIGHTMARE

Paul lies facedown on the ground beside my tower, tangled in jagged rose thorns. I walk toward him, compelled to move forward by some unseen force. I kneel on the hard ground and wrestle with the branches to help him sit up. When he faces me, I see his face is scratched and bleeding. "Rapunzel?"

What is this? "Paul—? I thought you died?"

"I did. I died because you forgot me."

"I have never forgotten you!"

"You have forgotten me and left me behind. I love you and you have left me behind." He reaches toward my face and strokes my cheek. I cover his hand with my own, wanting to hold onto this apparition forever.

"No—I—I saw you fall—I know she killed you!"

"You have forgotten me and allowed hatred to rule in your heart!"

"No!"

The pounding on the door wakes me from the nightmare. It is still black outside and I can't see anything but shades of darkness around me. Then the door bursts open with a candle held before the rough face of a man I can't remember seeing before. He is dragging a maid with him whom I don't recognize and he shoves her at me. "Lady Rapunzel! You will ready yourself at once to meet King Purnell and Lord Col."

"What—?" But he slams the door behind him before I can ask what this is about. I look at the strange maid who seems afraid. "Where is Plesencia? Do you know what's going on?"

"I don't know anything, your ladyship, just that I was sleeping when he crashed into my room and almost ripped my arm off to get me here." She tries to light the candle on the stand beside my bed, but her hands are shaking and I must do it myself. She then goes to the trunk where my clothes are folded and selects something, but I can't focus enough to even realize what I am putting on. What could all this mean? I try to shake off the dream. I thought I was through with nightmares. All I know is that, as fast as I can get ready, I am in the Great Hall, giving a deep curtsy before the king and the lord, wishing that I knew why so many men have come out of their beds.

"Lady Rapunzel, you have been brought on this trip because you are betrothed to my son, is that not so?"

"That is why he said I was to accompany him."

This gives him pause. "Are you not betrothed?"

"I don't know, Your Majesty . . ." My words fumble, but I feel that at last, I must be honest about my true position. "Your son brought me to this island to help rescue his mother. I don't understand how I have helped him, but he says I am necessary and so I remain. He has said we are to be married, and everyone seems to accept that fact."

"Aren't you going to marry him?"

"He says I will once my period of mourning is over."

"How did I not know you were in mourning?"

"Her mourning is of a peculiar kind, Father." I hear the door creak open as Edmund joins. His boots thump across the stone floor as he hurries across the hall to stand beside me. Together we face the front of the table where the king and lord sit looking down from the raised platform, harsh lines crowding the face of the king, sorrow etched in the lord's face. "She was betrothed secretly and then her intended was killed. She was banished to live without the protection of those who raised her."

The king scrutinizes me. "Secretly betrothed? What kind of maid have you become ensnared by, my son?"

"The kind who has helped me find my mother, the queen. Her guardian was a horrible person—wicked. It was right for her to find her own way apart from the life she had known."

"What mischief did she learn at the knee of those who raised her, I wonder?"

"What do you mean?"

"It seems that her maid has been killed."

"Her maid?" Edmund says, as I gasp out, "Plesencia?"

"She was found this evening. The other maids say that you gave her the day?"

I try to swallow so I can speak. "I did. She wasn't feeling herself this morning. I gave her leave to rest and recover."

"She didn't go to rest; she went out to a tavern."

"Plesencia?" This doesn't sound like her at all.

"Did you know she was with child?"

"—*Plesencia?*" I can't seem to say anything else.

"Yes, she was found dead in a room there. It is obvious that she was trying to get rid of a babe she was carrying."

"What?" It feels as though I'm in a nightmare still.

"We found this in her possession." He holds out a necklace upon which is a vial. I recognize the necklace: it was the one from the High Queen I had given her that morning.

"I gave that to her."

"She didn't steal it?"

"No, of course not. She was a good servant and I wanted to do something for her, so I gave it to her."

"You admit you gave her a vial of poison?"

"No—" I try to breathe, but it's difficult. "I was told the vial was full of a potion that would cause great love, but I—I had no need for it. I don't understand—what was it?"

"It killed the child she was carrying, and killed her."

I feel dizzy and I must find somewhere to be sick. My stomach heaves and I splatter vomit on the floor, which splashes onto my gown, my shoes, and narrowly misses Edmund. He reaches over to catch me, but two guards come to grab me instead.

"What's going on?" Edmund demands to know as the maid who brought me here runs out of the room and returns with rags to clean up the mess I've made.

"Rapunzel is going to be hanged for her part in the murder of her maid. Some might think maids don't matter, but she was the mother of a child, and if she was murdered, then Rapunzel must pay."

"You can't be serious! Rapunzel wouldn't kill her maid."

"No? Then why does my apothecary say the maid was poisoned by that vial?"

"I don't know, I don't know, but Rapunzel would never hurt anyone. And she loves—loved Plesencia. I saw them together, the girl was like a friend to Rapunzel."

"She was my friend." I am hollow and I feel nothing but the pressure on my arms where the guards are holding me tight. How can Plesencia be dead? How can something I gave her have killed her?

"Take her to my dungeon!" the lord cries with force, tears streaming down his red face.

⊂⊇⊃

I THOUGHT VISITING Fenella in the dungeon was horrible, but being in one by myself is much worse. I know nothing but the cold dampness that seeps into my bones, the rotting smell of waste mixed with my own vomit that assaults my nostrils. I can barely eat when hard bread and murky water are delivered to me hours later. How long have I been on this wet, cold floor? The numbness that first captured me has fled and left terror in its wake. What is happening to me? Why don't I know how to prove I did nothing wrong? Did the High Queen give me a vial of poison instead of the love potion she claimed it to be?

I know better than to think that the wind that swirls toward me is natural. The witch arrives in the darkness with her bitter words to torment me. Her form floats, ghostlike, over the damp stones.

"Interesting that you shared the vial. I'm surprised you didn't use it for yourself. Don't you want to be in love and be happy, dearest Rapunzel?"

"I was in love, and I was happy. I don't know that I could ever be that again."

"And yet you were going to get married. Do you think he will still want you? Not the way you smell now."

"Probably not," I mutter.

"So why didn't you use the potion?"

I stare up at her. "You would have allowed that?"

She cackles; my ears protest against the noise. "You think I would allow you to have a true love potion?"

"I never thought I would use it all. I want no part in potions and spells."

"You should have spilled it out."

"I would have if I had known it would kill—you would have killed me? You would have killed me like—" But I can't say her name. The searing pain shoots through my heart and again I struggle to breathe.

"I hate to see you like this," she clucks as she mocks me.

"Don't you want to see me in pain?"

"Of course not!" she spits, "I want to see you back home, with me!"

"And if I don't go, you want me to die?"

"No!"

"Then why turn a love potion into poison?"

"It wouldn't kill you." She sounds as though she can hardly force herself to admit this.

"It killed Plesencia! Why wouldn't it kill me?"

"Because you are special, Rapunzel—you always have been. I made certain of that. I have great things in store for you, but you must be humbled, you must realize you need me and that what I have planned for you, for us, for the kingdoms is best. You need me!"

"So you would poison me? Almost kill me?"

"I would not have allowed you to be in a danger too great. She was weak, not made of the stuff of magic like you are."

"Oh, no—I'm not made of magic! I've been incarcerated by it, hunted by it, hurt by it, but it has no part in me."

"Tell yourself whatever you wish, child. One day you will see I am right and you will join me. If you join me now, I can see that you are free at once and leave this place behind."

"If I'm with you, I'll never be free."

"Then enjoy your prison, my dear. I will come to see you hang when it is time. Perhaps then you won't be so upset with me. You will cry for me to free you before this is over and accept—"

"Get out!" I scream and begin to sob.

<hr>

It's late when I hear Edmund come, and he brings light into my cold cavern. The dripping of water plinks nearby and his jaw clenches as he looks down on me. "They think you are guilty, Rapunzel."

"But why would I wish to kill her?"

"Because she was with child and it would disgrace the household."

I shake my head. I'm confused what a maidservant being unwed and pregnant would have to do with the honor of the household. "She was so thoughtful, so sweet. Do we know who the father of the child was?"

"Likely someone back in my father's court. The household staff is sworn not to mingle, but it happens sometimes. When it does, they are either made to marry or they are dismissed. Often, I am sad to say, it is the maid alone who is dismissed. It's impossible to know who the father is in such cases unless the woman tells."

"It's not fair."

"No, this world is rarely fair, Rapunzel. Do you sometimes wish you had stayed in your tower?"

Even though there are tears on my lashes I shake my head. "The witch was here," I find myself whispering.

"What?"

"The witch was here. She visits me, taunts me sometimes."

"Why didn't you ever tell me?"

Why didn't I? I don't know. I just shrug. I can't look up.

"Why did she come?"

"She wants me to know that she could save me from all of this. She caused the potion in my vial to change." I give an empty laugh that reverberates against the stones. "Even now she could save me from being hanged."

"Why did she do this to you?"

"So I would see how much I need her."

There is a long pause, but when I look up into his face, I see his lips are parting as though something pleasant has occurred to him. "But you don't need her—you need me."

"What do you mean?"

"I can save you. I have the power of my wish."

"But you said it costs you something each time you—"

"You think I would not gladly pay the price to set you free?" He looks almost angry as the candlelight quivers across his features. "Besides, I too want you to know that you need me." He smiles again and I feel something strange tug inside as he bends to kiss my lips. "I will not see you harmed." He starts to walk away.

"But Edmund, if you just make a wish anytime things go wrong, what kind of king will you be? Will your father be able to entrust his kingdom to you?"

"Who better than I? I can save you."

"I don't want you to—"

"It's too late, Rapunzel, it's as good as done."

Within an hour I've been set free. It's as though it never happened because Edmund wished that everyone would simply forget. They would forget Plesencia and her unborn child, they would forget the love potion that became poison. No one remembers I was in the dungeon and they seem to have forgotten an entire day. I don't know how many wishes Edmund will have to make on returning to his father's kingdom to erase Plesencia there, but I make him promise not to erase my memory of her. I don't ever want to forget someone who has been good to me. Edmund seems worn, but happy with his sacrifice. He pulls me into a room near the Grand Hall to kiss me before supper. He's gotten quite adept at keeping his sword out of the way when he takes me in his arms. I am startled by his passion, but he smiles and laughs, as though intoxicated by his heroism. I am grateful, but I find I am also afraid. I don't linger long in this thought but allow him to pull me along, back to have the evening meal with the company, our last one before we head onward once more.

The jester juggles roses this evening while telling of a girl who loved a beast. When he concludes his tale, he gives the roses to the queen and me. "It is good you are still with us, Lady Rapunzel. I had a dream last night that you were in danger, that you had fallen among the thorns." I stare into his dark, opaque eyes. "I am glad you are well. I'm excited to know the rest of your story—I will be seeing you again," and he bounds away. When I look down, I see that one of the thorns must have cut his hand; there is a drop of blood on the stem, but the flowers themselves are unbruised.

DESIRE

I have watched a change come over the queen as
we go to visit her sister; she flutters with excitement over greeting her kinswoman after such a long sepa-
ration. The country surrounding the castle is rich
farmland, the commoners seem healthy, and the few
dwellings I glimpse are well kept with robust animals strut-
ting about.

It seems the queen's father made a prudent match for
both his daughters, though her sister had the happier
marriage until now. We are greeted warmly on the cobble-
stones in the inner bailey by the family and several
servants. The two sisters embrace while servants collect our
things and take them up the stone staircase that leads into
the main building of the white stone castle. I smile to see
the sisters so happy.

I cannot tell by looking who is the elder. They are of
similar heights and coloring, though the lady is a bit heav-
ier. I know why right away. Behind her skirts hides a young
pair of tow-headed twins, while nearby five other children

wait to meet their kinsmen. These are just the youngest; several others are busy in lessons and other duties all around the castle. Lady Genevieve encourages the prince to meet with the captain of the guard, a man her family has trained from youth. This same man is now training three of her sons to fight.

"Isn't that unusual? Shouldn't they be training with another lord?" the prince asks.

"It is strange, but when my husband, the lord, became ill four years ago, I called our eldest back from where we had sent him to wait and see how his father fared."

"And how is my lord?" asks King Purnell, fully acquainted with the details of the long-standing illness of his brother-in-law and loyal lord.

"Neither better nor worse. He would like to see you at your pleasure, Your Majesty." She bows her head in deference, and I wonder how she feels about this man who imprisoned her sister for so long.

A beautiful young lady comes to meet the queen. Her curves are quite apparent by the way she has arranged her yellow surcoat so that its low neck rests on the rise of her breasts and her girdle sits on her full hips. Her velvety chestnut hair is uncovered in the way of many unmarried Ronan maids and plaited with golden ribbons. Her entire countenance is meant to please, but I find myself uneasy, though I don't know why until I see how she looks at Edmund.

"Your Majesty, Prince Edmund," her ladyship nods to the king and son, "I present my daughter, Beatrix."

Beatrix comes forward, a sultry smile splitting her lips just a bit.

"Oh, good," says the queen as she steps forward to intercept the young lady. "Rapunzel, my son's betrothed, has been without companionship since we began this long journey through the kingdom. I am happy you will be here to make her at home." This is somewhat true, I feel lost now that I no longer have Plesencia. She wasn't quite a proper lady-in-waiting, but I miss her so much I ache, especially when I think of the part I played in her death. I have had no desire to make any more friends since we left the castle where she died and all companionship has been unmanageable due to the brevity of each stay. I must say that my need for solitude has not helped matters.

Edmund smiles at his cousin and then follows a servant to where the knights are training. I try to smile, but I cannot feel it inside.

OUR FIRST MEAL in the Great Hall seems normal enough, but for the lack of the lord. The king takes over the lord's position and sits center, as he should, and the two sisters sit side by side to his left overlooking a large hall full of people seated at long hawthorn tables. Edmund has rearranged things so that he might sit next to the eldest of the brothers, all of whom seem to be acquainting him with the realities of knighthood without giving him a difficult time about his own lack of training. I am gratified to see he enjoys their company; I wonder if they remind him of the players.

The smacking of mouths is unending and I try to focus my thoughts on the meal, but I am distracted by the very direct gaze of Beatrix who is seated to my left. "The prince was so long away from his throne. However did you and my cousin become acquainted?"

How does one respond to such perusal? He found me working as a kitchen maid in a kingdom across the Illyan Sea? "We kept meeting in our travels."

"Oh, yes, I did hear he traveled for years as a troubadour, trying to discover his rightful heritage. So he met you in your father's kingdom?"

"No."

"Were you visiting your uncle or a lesser lord's kingdom?"

"No."

She bats her eyelashes, in feigned innocence. "Then, how did you meet?"

I blink my eyes and still my breathing. "He is the troubadour and tells the tale much better than I. I should think you would like to hear it from him."

"Quite so, but don't you think it beneath a future king to sing for his meal?"

"Indeed, a future king need never sing for his meal. But this future king sometimes chooses to gift us with a tale." I feel the stiff grin freeze on my face. "I am sure he would oblige you at the right time." I hope I am speaking the truth. He does so love to sing; perhaps he would not mind that I have given him the task of singing the tale that we have never shared even with the king and queen.

It is a simple thing to settle, though the look the prince gives me is odd before he takes up his lute. After all, how many princes sing their own tale? But on our travels I have heard him working this song out, arranging the tune, fixing the words in his mind, though never when he knew I was listening. He has hummed it for weeks with a faraway look, and I know him and how he works. He misses his nights of performing.

His voice and playing seem to intrigue all who listen, and soon they are enamored of their newly-found prince. With brevity, he opens by singing of his escape from Elias and then begins to weave the story of his search through the kingdom for his family. He tells of his first master and how he came to travel with the players once they played for the same lord. Along his journey, he sings of meeting a girl disguised as a kitchen maid, and later, a true lady of the court. I assume he is speaking of me, but I was never a lady at court—I was convinced to play one to help solve the mystery of the ruined slippers. Beatrix is staring at me now, her expression inscrutable. To me, she seems the real lady at court, scheming with ideas I don't wish to understand.

After his lengthy description of setting free his mother and bringing about the peaceful reunification of the king and queen with my help, he looks at me and sings of his proposal, but he sings as though I have already accepted. I feel flushed but cannot escape the many eyes staring at me. I wish I knew where I could go to find solitude; this crowd is unbearable!

I want to retire to my chambers as fast as possible, but Edmund whisks me away once the crowd begins to scatter. Suddenly, we are in an unlit room I have never seen before and he is kissing me. I can't catch my breath. I should be feeling delighted or a sense of thrill, but the thrill is tainted by fear. His story, the one he sang—was it about me? Has my silence in the recent weeks been taken for acceptance? I have tried to accept him and let him kiss me. Still, I never said I was his. His kisses become deeper, but I pull away, hoping he'll notice my reluctance. He pulls me in closer, and my passivity dissipates. "No!" I state in a firm voice, a swelling of panic bubbling up inside me. I know he has no intention to harm me, but would he allow his desires to overwhelm me? I will not be demeaned.

His look is confused as I push him away. I turn my head as he reaches for me. "I need to retire, Sir."

"Rapunzel—"

"Good night, Edmund."

He places his hands on my shoulders, willing me to look at him, "Rapunzel—"

"I am not some common wench, even if you did find me in the kitchen! Good night!" I spin and march off to my room where I send out all the maids so that I can cry in peace.

◦◦◦

Breaking fast with the queen is always pleasant, and her sister seems as genteel as she. But Beatrix changes the atmosphere when she comes into the long room with her younger sisters. She sits in the padded chair beside mine at a table adorned with glazed bowls of spiced figs and porridge. It's as though my porridge suffers for her presence. What is it about her? She acts pleasing toward everyone but me. I feel as though she smells something repugnant to her noble nose when she comes near, even though she gives the appearance of courtesy.

"I trust you slept well, my lady?" She smiles as I nod. "Your chambers have been often in use this summer. Of course, never anyone as dignified as the lady to marry the future king. I trust if there is anything you need you will let us know. We saw that you do not have your own maid."

The queen, overhearing our exchange, intervenes. "No, we are still searching for one that is to our liking for Lady Rapunzel. I'm sure you understand, Lady Beatrix, choosing one's maid is of a delicate and important nature." It pains me that she can't remember the sweet girl who served me during most of our trip.

"I do understand—particularly difficult if one has not done so before."

Queen Lefwenna either does not notice this or ignores it. "I, myself, was thrilled to find that my loyal maidservant had stayed with the king in my absence, serving ladies who visited His Majesty." She glances back in adoration at her old confidant, the dark-eyed woman who stands in attendance with the other maidservants. They stand against the stone wall below a tapestry which denotes her ladyship's genealogy back four generations.

"Oh, yes, dear Elizabeth has often helped me when we had to visit during your confinement. We are so glad to see her again." Lady Genevieve smiles long at the woman she remembers well.

Beatrix is not distracted in the least and turns to me with a slanted smirk. "Have you had to choose one before? What I mean is, do you know what to look for?"

I know what she means, and a fit of unfamiliar anger seethes inside me as I would like to tell her all about the past she wishes to know. Yes, I'd like to say, I had a very good maid until the witch poisoned her. Though I have never chosen my own, I have been a maid and so I should know how to choose one. But a quick glance at the queen stops my tongue. "I have experience with many maids. With Her Majesty's guidance, I believe I will do very well, thank you." Mustering as much decorum as I can, I resume my meal, and her needling questions at last come to an end. For now. I wish I could sigh in relief, but I know that it will be a temporary respite until she gets what she wants.

UNSEEN

*E*dmund seems preoccupied with all things related to knights during this visit and spends his day studying their routine in the outer bailey. I have no chance to see if he is put out by my behavior, but since I do not know if I have forgiven him yet, I am not going to seek him. Instead, I allow the younger sisters to show me their favorite haunts. This includes a visit to the gardens, a nearby wishing well, and at last the stables where I am confronted once again by large horses.

As they are bewildered by my reluctance to enter the stables, I try my best to explain. "I have ridden behind horses, but never upon one. They seem nice enough"—I try not to stammer—"to those who know them, but I never have."

"Well, we should remedy that at once. How can you become a queen if you have never ridden?" I am relieved that Gwynndolen, the second oldest, is so little like her sister. She has amber eyes, bright red hair and little patience for politics or sitting inside. As soon as we were done eating, Gwynndolen was the one to suggest the outing. The queen, Lady Genevieve, and Beatrix all declined in order to stay inside and work on needlepoint in her ladyship's sitting room. Gwynndolen rolled her eyes at her sister's back as she walked off with the older women.

I shake my head as I am pulled closer to the large building and Gwynndolen instructs one of the stable boys to fetch her favorite horse. "Early in our trip, the others went on a hunt," I remark.

"I suppose you could not because you don't know how to ride? That is a shame—hunts are very important. We have a great many horses—and even dogs that love a good hunt!"

I must look confused, so she enlightens me as to how royals enjoy working up a sweat by racing on horseback with dogs after some sort of prey. Her favorite hunt is after deer, as there are often many caught and—this last bit I know—a feast generally follows. "We've not had a hunt since father grew ill. Well, others have hunted, but not a large hunt called out by him." Her bright eyes cloud as her expression droops. "But that must change soon. We no longer expect him to get better and we must resume living."

She clips off the sad memories and turns to select a beautiful black creature. "This is the mare you should ride. She's gentle and I think you'll get along."

"Does she have a name?" I watch the way Gwynndolen holds the bridle and the nuzzling response of the mare as she strokes her nose.

"I don't name my horses."

Even so, the animal is special to her. She beckons me to

walk closer and I focus on Gwynndolen, ignoring my churning stomach. The horse seems to sense my reluctance and paws the ground in impatience, puffing out air through her mouth. Gwynndolen speaks in a low, steady tone and encourages me to do the same.

"It does not matter what you say so much as how you say it. You want your calm speech and manner to show her she can trust you."

Yes—but can I trust the beast to not crush me? I take a filling breath and find myself humming a low tune. The mare's ears cock to the side, listening, but still, I cannot look her full in the face. Gwynndolen nods to the stable boy, who hands me a carrot. I feel stupid as I look up at him. "You feed it to the horse, m'lady," he offers. I reach my hand out with something less than confidence and the horse snuffles my hand. Her lips pull back over massive, blunt teeth and she happily snatches it out of my hand, leaving a smear of drool clinging to me. I untuck my handkerchief from my bodice and wipe off the residue, but I smile at how happy the mare is. Completing the mouthful, she turns and nudges me, and I can't stop smiling as I feed her another carrot handed me by the stable boy. After this, we seem to get on well, and I even stroke her head a bit before heading in for the midday meal.

"You did quite well," Gwynndolen informs me as we head inside. The younger girls abandoned us earlier, so we walk alone.

"Do you think so?"

"I think so. May I ask how you have had so little dealings with horses?"

"I was brought up in a most unusual manner and had little dealings with anything or anyone but my guardian."

"Ah, I have heard of those who cloister their most promising daughters . . ." is all the young woman can say, but she shrugs with a light-hearted air despite her confusion. "Well, we have some of the best horses in all of Rona —the king himself says so—and we often supply him with horses for his cavalry when he has a need. Every few years, we take some as a tribute to the High King. I hope to go the next time." Her voice trails away and then she clears her throat. "So, while you are here, you should learn all you can." She eyes Beatrix before we find our separate places. "If you allow me to help you, no one will ever know about your lack of education."

Her offer of friendship humbles me, and I nod in assent. I have no wish to shame the family I might soon become a part of, and so I will endeavor to learn all I can from this kind young woman.

⚬⚬⚬

EDMUND REMAINS aloof the following day and I find myself alone, as the young ladies all have things to do and the queen is busy reminiscing with her sister. I begin poking around the castle, discovering too late that I have lost my way. This castle has been built on several times. The first, older part was wood, but as the lord's family grew wealthier, so did the building materials. The halls are twisty and confusing. A winding staircase leads me to a small room boasting two bookshelves filled with books, proving again what a rich lord we are visiting. I take the liberty to sit down on a hard bench to look through a few of the books but find myself becoming bored. I know the languages, and the words are telling me nothing new. Perhaps one day I'll return to the love of book learning, but for now, I must allow my feet and not my fingers to guide me.

At the back of the small room is a curious-looking door, half the size of the other doors in the castle. It opens outward at me revealing a small archway covered by the back side of a tapestry. With quiet steps, I walk into the next room and I hear strained breathing. My flesh prickles, but the door has closed behind me and I cannot get it back open. I move the tapestry aside and find I am in his lordship's sickroom. A strong odor assaults my nose. A pale woman with black eyes in a nun's coarse brown habit is attending him. She is just finishing spooning broth between his lips. She looks unsurprised by my appearance and waves me closer as she puts down the wooden bowl and spoon. She points to the fine porcelain basin as she picks up the rag from it and begins to wash his face. By instinct, I know to take the basin. She finishes her task, never speaking. She reminds me of Sister Agnes, though her manner is not the same.

How can I describe how Lord Colin looks? His skin should be pale from his bed-bound position, but it is flushed while his lips are grey. His head is covered in a shock of white bristled hair, and his eyes, unseeing, are grey, all but transparent except for the black specks of his pupils. His withered body is smothered by several heavy blankets while his body moves restlessly beneath them. His naked arms are covered with wiry black hairs that stick out over the top of them. At long last, the sister is satisfied, and she takes back the basin. Placing both bowl and rag in it, she motions me to follow her out of the room, using the discreet door I used instead of the grandiose one at the other end of the chamber.

"Thank you, my lady," she says after closing the door behind us.

"I am sorry to have interrupted. I never meant to intrude. I got lost and—"

"I understand. As a child, I used to explore the castle and often lost my way."

"You grew up here?"

"I am his lordship's sister." Her low voice is raspy, as though seldom used.

"I see," I say—but I don't.

"When he became unwell, I returned to nurse him."

I nod and give a half-smile. "Have you been here for his entire illness?"

"Most of it."

"That must be difficult—four years away from the convent."

Her black eyes seem to shiver. "We are meant to serve. I serve here. I still have much time to pray and fast, and I know that I am useful."

"Why is he still unwell?" I wish the words back as soon as they are said, but the woman gives me an odd expression, as though she is thinking about something pleasant that is beyond me.

"It is as our Lord wills."

I believe she is talking of her God. I nod, feeling ill, and leave her presence at once, hoping to shake off the feeling of dread that has enveloped me since intruding upon the sickroom.

⌒⊱⊰⌒

EDMUND FINDS me after the evening meal. "I only have to locate a garden if I wish to find you."

But do you wish to find me? I don't voice my doubts, but he senses something is wrong. "Are you better tonight?"

"Better than what?"

"The other night . . . ?"

It isn't an apology. He wants to know if I have reconciled myself to his actions. "Will you allow yourself such liberty again?"

He places his hands on my shoulders and looks at me; it is his kind expression and I want to believe it is the true Edmund. "I am sorry I worried you," he sighs as he looks at me with his unblinking dark eyes. "I suppose we should marry soon."

"Why?"

"Little Rapunzel, so naïve, don't you know how I want you?" His kiss is soft, and when he pulls away I taste sweetness. "Do you understand how much I have to restrain myself with you?"

I understand wanting; the desire my Paul stirred in me had all but bewildered me. But Edmund's passion frightened me. With him, I felt unsafe.

As though reading my very thoughts, he touches my cheek, his thumb gliding along my jawline. "I will not hurt you. I will work harder to hold myself back." His lips meet mine again, his kisses softening my yielding mouth. His hand travels down to the small of my back, pulling me into his hard chest. His kiss then becomes firmer and I now feel a quickening inside me. The desire I had only felt for my beloved has reawakened, but with it a conflict. I had been sure of my beloved; he had not touched me until I felt safe with him. But Edmund? Edmund intrigues me, stretches me, but I still feel . . . I'm unnerved by him. How can a man who has but to wish something into being develop the discipline to withhold from himself the thing he desires? It's disloyal of me to think this way. Didn't he save me with his wish?

But then he releases me. His breathing seems a bit strained, but his self-congratulatory smile lifts his features. "I will not endanger your virtue, my love." Once more he kisses me, and then he is gone, leaving me alone in the night.

LESSONS

The mare is tall, and sitting on her with my knee hooked over a knob on the sidesaddle, I feel certain I will plummet to the ground and be trampled. Gwynndolen is convinced I will be fine and walks around the yard holding the bridle gently while I clench the reins so hard my own hands ache.

"Try to breathe and relax. Feel the rhythm of the horse beneath you—"

"I do, that's why I'm so scared."

"Oh, Rapunzel, I wouldn't let any harm come to our future queen!"

I nod and try to concentrate on the sound of the horse's hooves. Clip-clop, clip-clop, I close my eyes. Clip-clop, clip-clop, I take a deep breath. Clip-clop, clip-clop, I feel myself beginning to move in the saddle, moving into a rhythm with the horse. Clip-clop, clip-clop, I open my eyes and focus ahead, starting to enjoy the ride.

Gwynndolen is now moving faster, the sure-footed mare following her lead. The pace is a trot on the even ground, and I feel exhilarated. Perhaps this is the joy my beloved felt when he rode out to meet me. I take a deep breath as I remember. I will always think of the sound of his horse and the love in his face when he spoke of the hunt. I know I will always miss him.

I turn my thoughts and look at Gwynndolen when she settles us into a walk. "Have you arranged a hunt yet? Perhaps we could have one for the king and prince."

"I've spoken to mother, and I think she will. It is time and we are desperate for a reason to feast and celebrate . . ." But her eyes falter, and she slows to walk.

"I saw your father. I am so sorry. How did he become ill?"

"It was nothing at first, just a bad cough. It was near the Christ Mass and he insisted on one last hunt before our fasting began. Even after that, he only had a stubborn fever, but then he began getting dizzy, and that horrible far-away look—! He says he feels like he's flying, but he's so sick now, and his mind is . . . He was once hale, so strong, the equal of any knight, but now . . ." A single tear splashes down her face. She looks down too late. I have seen her pain and know I must find a way to help. But how can I help stop the slow death of a man? I am no healer.

⊂⊇⊇⊃

EDMUND IS RIGHT: I return to the garden over and over again. No matter where we go or how long we stay, I must find my way to the garden, perhaps looking for the peace I once found.

The plants growing here are reminding me of all the

other gardens of my life. My mind conjures up the image of the garden behind the cottage the witch and I shared. It was filled with her favorite plants of life and destruction. Of course, here I find the weed-like horehound she would never grow to ward off poisons, the leafy laurel to promote healing, the thorny blessed thistle to ward off plague. I take a few more steps and find the lovage plant that promotes healing reaching up with its pointy leaves and its tiny yellow flowers just now budding. Beyond that are the various mints to encourage all sorts of health and wellness. It's not that my witch didn't use some of the other plants I see planted here; she grew the same ground ivy I see entwining itself around the parsley. The foxglove and fennel she also had uses for. But some things I choose not to remember, and others she chose not to tell me. But this plant to my right, its yellow flower and odd-shaped leaves reaching out like small hands from the stem . . . Something strikes me about its position, as though it was not intended to grow among the spiky rosemary and large umbels of the white-flowering angelica. A strong odor emanates in the sun, but it is mixed with the scents of the other pungent herbs. Nostalgic smells overwhelm me and I lean back, my head feeling light and heavy at once.

I shake my head and depart from the grounds. I have been out too long in the bright sun.

⚬

MY HEART still reacts in a strange way as I mount the black mare. I want to connect with her, and Gwynndolen must see this in my face.

"Talk to her and pat her neck. Have you ever had a pet, Rapunzel?"

Would my feline mother count? Perhaps before I knew she was my mother, but then I didn't think of her as my pet after my beloved fell. "I once had a cat." I feel myself stroke the mare with a sense of awe. Whereas before I was overwhelmed by how huge and strong they were, now I see the majesty in their might, the beauty in their power. I pat her and she jerks her head to glance back at me. My heart jumps, but I pat her again and whisper in a low tone something I remember Edmund saying to his horse when I still knew him as the troubadour.

I feel Gwynndolen observing me. When I look her way, she has a small smile, almost an intangible secret on her lips. "My father used to say that when he was training a horse."

"A lord who trains horses?"

"It is what we are known for. Of course, he hasn't since he grew ill." The smile pulls down on her lips. "I think he must miss the horses. How could he not? You feel it now, too, or very soon will. A horse can know your thoughts, your needs. But he's been away from them so long . . ." Her voice trails off, which seems incongruent with her nature. She snaps back and takes the reins, handing them to me. "I will walk alongside, but you direct her. She will hear you."

For a time she talks me through the different ways of guiding a horse with my hands and my seat. Evidently, it is easier to maneuver when straddling a horse, as using your knees is much more effective. Gwynndolen tells me this with an impish grin; she enjoys wearing clothing that allows her the freedom to sit astride. But a proper lady can ride sidesaddle and still direct the horse, though it does take practice to develop the skill.

Practice is exhausting, and I retire to my room well-worn. But when I lay down to rest until the evening meal, all at once I remember the plant I saw: henbane!

I jerk myself upright from the bed and look around me, as though expecting to see the witch's face. Has she put this thought in my mind? I look around me, expecting a shimmering image to stare back at me, but nothing appears—no visual apparition, no rising wind, no voice cackling through the silence. I dash out of the room, hoping I know what I am doing.

HER MAJESTY HAS JUST FINISHED CONFESSING, and I wish I could confess and be rid of the horrible dread that consumes me. But I will be guilty if I do not try to right this wrong.

"Rapunzel—?" Her smile falters, head leaning toward me. "My dear, are you quite well?"

"No, Your Majesty, I am not. I need your counsel."

"Of course, my dear, of course." She places a hand around my shoulder, giving a gentle squeeze of confidence. "Let us retire to my chamber."

"If it pleases Your Majesty, I would rather it be to the gardens."

"The gardens? If that suits you better . . ." But she blinks.

Once outside, I take a shaky breath. "Since arriving I

have come to care for your sister's family, and it worries me that his lordship is unwell and wavers between health and death."

A sheen of tears mists the queen's eyes as she nods.

"I have wished I was able to help his lordship."

She squeezes my right shoulder once again and takes my left hand in her own.

"I happened upon him the other day in his chamber by mistake. I had taken a wrong turn and came through a servant's entrance and found his sister, the nun, medicating him with a broth. I have worked before alongside a ministering nun, Sister Agnes, who used herbs and plants to heal people and she taught me a bit of what she knew." I take a deep breath as we walk among the herbs. "But before I knew her, I knew someone else who used plants to harm people, to make them ill and sometimes to prolong their illness. Your Majesty, you know I have no desire to slander anyone, but I have found a plant growing among the herbs that has but one purpose: to harm." I show her the plant, and as the air is still warm, the strong odor is present. "I smelled this when I saw his lordship, and I fear the worst. I did not know who else to tell."

The queen leans down and snaps off a flowering stem that she hides in her girdle. "You did well, Rapunzel. We will speak to her ladyship and the king. You may need to as well, my dear—it may be essential."

I nod, feeling ill.

❧

THE EVENING MEAL is enough to make me wish I were ill. First, I am again near the vigilant Beatrix, who continues to eye me and speak of things she must sense will prove my inferiority. I have noticed how she is not just watching me, but Edmund, who is oblivious to both of us as long as there is someone near to discuss stories of gallantry. Perhaps he is composing another grand song, but I am tired of feeling —I don't know!—this feeling I cannot name. It's as though he knows he has what he desires and—

I hate this twisting in my middle as they pass more plates, hunks of meat passed around with gobs of fat clinging. The vegetables swirl in front of me and I run from the room, finally sick. The vile taste burns the back of my throat and I heave until I am free of the acidic bile. I shiver when I turn and see the lord's sister watching me from the shadows.

"Are you unwell?"

I step backward, my back now against the outer wall of the hall. She steps around my vomit and touches my forehead. "Unwell." She shakes her head as she clicks her tongue. "Perhaps you ate something that does not agree with you. Perhaps you saw or smelled something you should not have." Her eyes bore into mine and her fingers press hard up into my scalp under my wimple where her scratch will remain undetected. I try to turn from her, but she snaps my head back, and though she is shorter than me, she manages to use her surprising store of strength to trip me into my own sickness. The sudden motion and smell prompt me to get sick once more and I hear her calling as I retch, the scratch in my scalp burning, and I black out, face down in the filth.

EVIL

I awake shaking with chills, a poultice on my chest. I see a dark shadow in the corner and scream as the nun comes forward—but my voice is frozen, I cannot speak a word. She smiles and puts a finger malevolently to her lips. "Be still, little one, and you will be well soon. This poultice I have prepared just for you, to help relieve you of what you fear."

The spots before my eyes distort her image as she comes nearer. Where is the queen? I told her the truth! Where is she?

Just as the woman gets to my bedside I hear a loud yowl and Cat springs forward to swipe at the woman and bite her. The woman jumps back with a yelp, but her thick woolen habit has kept her from any real harm. Cat now flies to my bed and stands guard, hissing each time the woman moves. I fight to remain alert but feel myself losing track of time. At last, the woman leaves with a curse. Cat turns to me as I summon my strength to fling the poultice from me. Just then, the chamber door is flung open, and

Edmund and the queen rush in with two armed knights. Once Edmund and the knights see there is no one but myself and the cat, Edmund commands them to search elsewhere. I have no strength to sit up or even to call out to Cat who licks me once on my cheek before lighting on my bed and jumping out a window. Did my mother just kiss me? I wonder as I stare after her, limp on the bed.

"Rapunzel, my love!" Edmund says, but I feel too weak to answer. "Where is that witch of a nun? Gwynndolen said she saw you become ill and told her maid to get something to help you. When the maid found you, the nun said you would be fine in her care and for the maid to leave. I thought to check on you in the morning, but Mother was concerned. She confided what you had said about the plant. We went at once to the apothecary, who knew the plant and warned the king to capture the nun at once."

I'm confused—if they have an apothecary, shouldn't he have been tending Lord Colin all along? My mind swirls as the queen steps forward and kisses my hand. "Poor, dear girl, what has happened to you?" I struggle to speak. "I became ill and she was helping me along," I manage to murmur at last, pointing my chin in the direction of the discarded poultice.

"My poor, poor girl." She pats my hand again as the apothecary comes to my aid.

Edmund gives his head a violent shake. "She will pay for this!"

His mother nods. "She will—but first, they must find her. Why not use your energy to that end, my son?"

The apothecary offers me some water but senses my resistance. He chuckles good-naturedly and takes a sip to prove the water is untainted. "My name is Clement, and I understand your mistrust. In the beginning, I tended the lord. But when his sister came, he insisted none but she tend to him. He never would have me after the Christ Mass, though I often wondered what I had done to offend. I suppose she said something to the lord to distance us."

I take a sip of the cool water and then sink back into the pillows, drifting dreamlessly until morning, knowing that it will all be sorted by then. Perhaps by then, I will care again.

MORNING COMES, and mornings after it, while I replenish my strength. It takes me a week, and in that time the lord's sister is found dead, having killed herself with her own store of henbane. The lord is still weak when we leave, but he promises a hunt the next time we visit. He has a few lucid moments, but the madness of the poison has altered him forever, they say. Perhaps I should have left him alone —but no, this thought is wrong. His family needs him, even if he is not the hale and hearty father they adored. Gwynndolen promises to take him every day to the stables, and it is where they hope he will be happiest.

THE WAY HOME

I am impatient for something, but I cannot name it. I am road-weary and long to return to the king's court where I feel I might sit for a time and decide which road my life should take. The longer we have traveled, the more confounded I have grown. The queen seems to sense my irritability and asked the king yesterday while we rode in the carriage how much longer we will be traveling. After the king replied it would not be long, she smiled at me and patted my hand. "You see, my dear, this is the last castle we are to visit, then we will go home and prepare for your wedding."

It is midsummer and I am hot, longing to be away from people altogether. I have spent so much of my life in solitude that though I enjoy this company, I feel that I am being smothered as I'm always surrounded. I give her a small nod and take comfort as I look out the carriage's window. Off in the distance, I spot some yellow and brown flowers, sunflowers growing wild in a field. I take comfort in the sight and try to relax. Soon we will return. I will make my decision and know what to do.

We go through the customary greeting with this castle's lord and lady. They show us the castle and take us to dinner, which we eat outside in honor of the sun as it is the longest day of the year. The people dance in a circle around the bonfire that has been lit and all the girls are adorned with yellow flowers. I let them adorn me, too, but I wish I could refrain without offending someone. Too much of what is being done reminds me of the celebrations the witch would have every year in our garden when I was young. She would harvest the herbs on this day for extra potency and chant her strange words. Though I enjoyed the celebration when I was very little, as I grew older, it seemed as though there was a root of bitterness in her celebration. She was harvesting the herbs for some angry purpose, she was dancing with a fury, she was contemplating something sinister. It is late before we go to our rooms and the sun is setting at last.

❧

LATE AT NIGHT, I startle awake. I hear something stirring in my guest chambers and feel a thump on my bed. "Are you awake, daughter?"

Her voice is as it always has been, feline, mystifying.

I sit up and stare at her green eyes glowing in the dark. I am grateful for the full moon by which I can just make out her outline. "Am I your daughter?"

"Yes." She circles around, picking out her spot, and

then settles down. She nestles into the thick bedding and begins grooming herself. "Did you never guess?"

I shake my head no, though I knew something about her was familiar, connected to me.

"You were my first-born, my one child. Your father and I were so young, just beginning our lives together."

I lick my lips, hesitating. "What of him do you know? Did the witch punish you both?"

"He died when you were small a few years after the witch took you and transformed me. She let me find out. She puts me where she wishes and then lets me ramble at will. Twenty years now I have roamed trying to break her spell, break her hold over you, but I have not found the way."

I stare at the feline before me. "Why did you steal from her? How could you not know you would lose me?" The witch used to spend our evenings before the fire telling me story after story. As I grew, I realized at last that the stories she was telling were her own—and many of them told of my origins, if I could unravel the common thread. Always, there was a woman who either sent her husband to steal or came to steal herself. She took what wasn't hers, and the price she paid was the child she carried. Me. It doesn't matter to me which of the witch's stories are true, only that my mother's desires cost my freedom.

"I was greedy and selfish. I thought hurting her would hurt no one else . . ."

"You hurt me."

"I know. I am so sorry." She blinks, her head hanging low, very un-catlike in her remorse.

"Why did you tell her of Paul?" I swallow hard and try to speak past my unforgiving swollen throat.

"She used me, and I was not as crafty as I thought. She suspected the truth before she put me in your tower, Rapunzel. Once I was there, she drew it out of me, though I tried to remain silent."

I nod in silence, trying to accept this, wondering if I can trust her. "Will I ever be free of the witch? Will I ever be able to know what to do with my life?"

"Your indecision has little to do with the witch or me. It is something every person must face, choices to determine your course in life. Rapunzel, you have been searching long enough since you left her tower; it is time to find your home."

"And what of you?"

"I must finish living out this curse before I am allowed to find a home. But when I do, will you forgive me and take me in?" She leans towards me, and I rub beneath her chin. Her scratchy tongue licks me once.

I want to say "yes"—but I'm not sure I can. Was the Paul in my dream right? Is my heart full of hate? Can I forgive or am I more like the witch than I know? I stare at Cat and I wonder what her true eyes look like. I wonder what it would be like to have grown up with such a mother.

When dawn approaches, I realize she has left again—but instead of missing her, I begin to hope for the next time we meet again. Perhaps curses will be broken, not just the kind that transformed her into a cat, but the kind that threatens to keep my heart hard.

A BANQUET HAS BEEN MADE in the king's honor at this final castle and we are seated at the head table before the lord's court. The Great Hall is familiar in its similarity to all of the other halls in castles that I have come across. At either end of the long rectangular room are two large empty fireplaces. Suspended from the ceiling are three wrought iron chandeliers holding dripping candles. There are also candelabras blazing on each table so that the light smell of beeswax mingles with that of food. Lined up lengthwise are two rows of five long tables set with metal goblets and wooden trenchers. Our head table is set up on a platform so that the lord and the king can view who sits before them. The servants bring in heaps of food: hearty stews, savory meat pies, salted beans, sweetened pears and plums, bread, pasties of fish, heathen cakes, toast rounds, smoked fish, and shelled nuts. The eating begins in the early evening and continues late as the sun sets, chins wag, and I grow bored.

Though the food is good, the conversation wearies me; I have no desire to learn any more of the politics of the nearby lands. I know such things are vital and I tell myself to listen, that if I am to become Edmund's wife I must at least attempt to understand what is entailed in the running of a kingdom . . . But my mind drifts and I watch as the musicians take their places to begin serenading the large throng.

Tables are cleared from the hall and people break into dance, lining up in long rows, following rules and steps I still don't know. I have watched dancing many times by now and I find it fascinating and beautiful, the weaving in and out, the coquettish smiles young maidens throw their partners. Though the touching seems no more than hand to hand, more than one woman becomes flushed. I can see many of the men take this opportunity to show their preferences. I look over at Edmund with hope; maybe this time he will notice how I long for him to teach me. This would be a wonderful way for me to understand better how I feel about him.

As has happened each time dancing has begun at any banquet, Edmund does not see me. This time he, his father, and the lord are too deep in conversation about the concern of the trade in goods across the Illyan Sea. The queen recognizes my distress, however, and moves to her son's side, nudging him in my direction.

"Rapunzel, would you care to dance?" He bows a bit at the waist after rising and holds out his hand for me.

I feel my face heat. "I don't know how, Your Highness."

"Well, then, come with me and we will see if you don't make a quick study."

I follow behind Edmund off the platform to observe, and that is when I see him: my beloved, across the hall from me.

Paul.

Paul is dancing without expression with a fine-looking maiden. I blink and try to think. It cannot be my love—I know it cannot be he. Paul was taken from me, thrown by the witch from my tower to perish, while I have been pushed into this wilderness to make my own way. I blink again, but his image remains before me. He is real, or at least his body is, though his blank face is a puzzle to me. As the music finishes, I cross to meet him, forgetting that I have no right to leave my partner without being excused. At once, Edmund follows to detain me, but I shake him off and continue to pursue the one I love. I reach him, out of breath, not caring about the commotion I have caused in the court of onlookers.

"My beloved, how are you here?" I beam at him, taking both his hands in mine and staring straight into his face.

All I receive is that vacant stare. Though I have taken his hands, ones that once reached for me, though he is looking into my face with eyes that once adored me . . . now he stares, a disoriented, dull expression on hardened features.

"Rapunzel, what are you doing?" Edmund is at my elbow, his question hurried. He is trying to hasten me from my beloved.

"Paul, don't you know me? I am Rapunzel, the maiden you sought to free from her tower."

My love looks from my face to Edmund's in confusion.

Edmund reaches out for me. "Rapunzel, who do you think he is?"

"This is Paul."

"You told me your love was dead."

"And so I thought he was, Edmund, yet here he stands . . ." But even as I say these words, a stone falls upon my stomach. My beloved does not know me. His hands lie like dead fish in my hands. He is polite and does not remove them, he does not turn away, but he does not know me and remains silent before me. I know the answer to my question, but I must ask: "Don't you know me?"

"No, my lady, I do not, and I think you must not know me."

"But I do, you came and rescued me—well, you tried to, but I thought you had died when the witch pushed you—"

"Witch?" This brings a near-smirk to his face.

"Yes, the one who kept me imprisoned—"

"My lady, there are no witches on this island, not since they were done away with long ago. There are only fools who believe such foolish things. I am sorry, but I am not your love and you do not know me." He bows with respect at the waist and I realize he is leaving me.

Through a dam of tears, I see the colors of the dancers shimmering as I turn to leave the hall. Without thought for how it will affect the royal family, I run to my chamber and shut the door, falling on my bed, weeping as I have not wept since leaving Dorothea's home in the Dark Wood.

THE SOUND BEGINS SOMEWHERE inside my head. Then there is a moaning of the wind, I think, but it grows louder until I can hear her laughing. I run to the window, a fierce gale shrieking in the night with the witch's laughter. "So, he has rejected you!" she crows, "Can't even remember the one he was willing to die for."

"What have you done to him?"

"I have been merciful. I have given him what he most needed: his mind."

"You have stolen the memory of our courtship."

"Are you so sure?"

I lean out the window. The wind rushes around my bare head, tangling my hair. "He could not even see me though he was looking at me."

"That is the world of men. They see you but do not see you. I have warned you but you would not listen." The clouds in the dark sky seem to form an outline of her image. "My sweet Rapunzel, now do you understand?"

"No, I don't! I understand that the one thing I had you have stolen. He may not remember me now, he may not be able to see me now, but I will remember him as the first person in this world who loved me and tried to rescue me. I'll not forget that—and that you cannot steal from me."

"There is nothing for you now. Come back to me. Live as we lived before." Her voice is a screech in the wind, and I can hear her desperation.

"You cannot make me go back." It is a realization. Though she can torment me, she cannot make me do anything. I am my own person and I am escaping her grasp. She is not as all-powerful as I once thought. "You cannot make me go back. My life is my own and you have no place in it. Leave me now!"

The storm wails one last time; then it begins to die. I do not have her powers, but I have my own, and I know now what I must do.

FORGETTING

*P*aul finds me waiting, stroking his horse in the stables the next morning. I would know his mare anywhere, though I have never seen her before. The moment I snuck into the stables, fighting my fear of the large creatures, I looked over the different horses and only two stood out. One was soot black and beautiful, but she had a haughty toss of her head. There was nothing tender about her, and I did not feel any affinity between us. His mare, however, is a gentle grey with soft black spots on her hind end and a white stripe down her nose. I remember how his voice dipped as he spoke of her strength and grey beauty. Though the other horses whinnied and made unsettled noises as I walked by their stalls, she turned and nuzzled me, as though she had always known me.

I know I must smell and look awful, having slept here all night. It is not the reunion I would have imagined had I thought such a thing was possible, but it was all I could think of to find him. He sees me and begins picking out his riding tack hanging nearby; he must be setting off soon.

"My lady, what are you doing here? I am sure your betrothed is looking for you, and the king and queen will soon be after. This is no place for a lady."

"You think I am a lady?"

He looks me over with his hazel eyes, but his hands continue to work as he saddles his mare. "You appear to be one, though a bewildered one given your conduct last night."

I ignore his comment. "And what are you?"

"Just a servant of the lord."

"A hunter?"

"At times—most often a knight who protects these lands." His mouth tips. "—But of course, you must know all that, given our intimate connection."

His jest, meant to prickle, stabs me with pain. It instead reminds me of the gentle way he would tease me. "We never spoke of your livelihood. We spoke of our beliefs, our desires, the hunt, some battles you'd been in, daily chores . . . For the past year I have wished I'd pressed you for more details, but I knew nothing of men—"

"Ah—because you lived in a tower guarded by a witch? Tell me, how did I get past this hideous creature?"

I look at him, wondering if my plan is so great after all. "Please, don't mock me, sir."

He looks away from me, uncomfortable with my words. "You are very beautiful, my lady, and I am honored that you would mistake me for someone you loved. You must hear how ridiculous"—his eyes dart around the stables —"and dangerous this sounds." His mare snorts as though sensing his discomfort.

"I suppose it does seem strange, and I wouldn't

endanger your standing with the lord or the king for anything, but—" I look at him, arrested by a new thought. How had he come to be on this island, so far from my tower? And though he now speaks the same language as the people of Rona, his accent is clearly from the Northlands. "How long have you been this lord's knight?"

"Perhaps a year."

"And before that, whom did you serve?"

His cocky grin slips a fraction. "Another."

"Where?"

"In another kingdom."

"Doing what?"

His gaze hardens. "The same thing I do here, I'm sure."

"You're sure? But you don't remember—do you?"

"A man's mind is not like that of a woman's. It is not crowded with details—"

"I'm not asking for details. You don't remember anything before this last year, do you?"

He looks away and shifts his footing as the mare looks back at me. "I remember my childhood, learning my trade . . . And then I remember being here. I recall enough. No witch has tricked me, if that is what you are implying."

I watch him, knowing that the rest of the grounds will soon stir. "Why did you come here so early this morning?"

"I have a great journey to make on my lord's behalf."

"I thought you weren't a messenger."

His sigh is weighted, but he answers. "I am not, but the message will take guarding. I am a servant, my lady; I do what I am bid to do." He turns to finish readying his mount.

"Without question."

This doesn't seem to sit well with him. "My lady, is there something you want from me?"

I strive to remain calm, to push down the emotions that threaten to take control, but the tears begin. "I want you to remember me—to remember us."

"I cannot, so I'd best be on my way—" He begins to mount, and then hesitates. "Will you be quite well?"

I try to shake off the tears, but I can't; they seem to keep coming. After all of the magic I have encountered in this world of men, is there nothing I can do to break this spell? "Please, you must try to remember me."

He un-gloves one hand and touches my right cheek, bewildered. "Are these tears for me?"

"They are for you, for the one who heard me singing and came to free me."

He leans towards me then. For a moment, I wonder if he remembers something, but he whispers, "I am sorry I cannot remember you, maiden, for the man who wins your heart is truly blessed." He kisses me, just a brush of his lips and I begin crying harder. I lean on his chest and begin to weep with abandon, not thinking of the red-faced mess I will become. I wonder if I will rust his chain mail. I am shamed by my display and before he can say another word, I rip myself away from him and run to the castle gardens.

DECISIONS

Time moves forward though I wish it would stop. As the queen promised, we have returned to the king's castle, but I have not been able to decide. I know I must choose now. I must make up my mind, but how? Should I leave here and roam again, or accept Edmund and forget my love? If I roam again, I will leave knowing forever the witch has won. If she has, then I will live alone for the entirety of my life. I feel like one of those waves by the queen's shore. As soon as I have made up my mind to marry Edmund, I fall back to questioning how to undo the spell on my beloved. Then I shake myself and try again to decide that I should marry Edmund.

I have spent days trying to decipher what I can do to cause him to remember all he has forgotten. But I have only to look at those around me who have no memory of my sweet maid Plesencia. Now that we have returned and Edmund has used the power of his wish, even her family has forgotten her existence. No one but he and myself remembers there was ever a child.

I don't like to think Edmund and the witch are simi-lar, but I know if he can cause such a blank in the memories of those who loved Plesencia, then there is no hope for my love to fight against the wiles of the witch. There is nothing I can to do to cause my love to remember me. I find myself listless and stagger through the castle. I feel like I should want to be away, I should want to leave and find the road and travel on forever. But instead, I stumble around, the sound of my gown drag-ging behind me. I cannot let go, but neither can I hold on anymore. If I let go I will find I was the only one holding on, the only one remembering. But if I hold on, I will never be free. Free to do what? my aching heart wonders. Day after day there is no answer, but I retreat to the gardens less and less and instead begin to haunt the chapel.

I go inside but never cross myself, for I do not wish to play the hypocrite. I never give a confession or say a word to the priests who would attend me if I but smiled at them. I don't know what I believe, I want to sit and have someone explain to me what I should do now.

I find myself praying, hoping this God who gave peace to Adeliza, who gave freedom to the queen, will find some way to reach me. What if he is worth trusting? What if he can help me find some way, to show me what I should do? I don't know if I should trust him, I don't know if it would be best, but part of me wants him to break through this fear in my heart and help me move forward.

It is weeks of this routine before the queen finds me one afternoon. I should be preparing to become a bride, since harvest time is coming soon—but instead, I am kneeling at the altar before a beautiful fresco of the birth of Christ.

"My child." Her voice is low and quite near; I had not heard her coming in my listless reverie. "What troubles you?"

No one has ever spoken to me of the night I went after my beloved—no one but Edmund. "I don't know."

"Rapunzel." She lifts my chin with the tip of her finger, causing me to look into her beautiful dark eyes. Today she has cast aside her wimple and pillbox and has her hair braided and wrapped around her head. I realize with a start it is the first time I have seen her hair, a beautiful auburn with grey touching its locks in a light caress. "Please confide in me. The priests say you come daily, but that you never say a word to them. What burden weighs on you? Is it marrying Edmund?"

I'm ashamed it's been weeks since that night in the lord's hall. I should have come to some decision by now. The one thing Edmund said to me was "It is in the past. You are mine now." He kissed me hard after that, but I know he has seen my swollen eyes, he knows I still mourn for my forgetful love. Edmund has not taken out his lute for me since, and we almost never find time to be alone.

"I should not marry your son, my lady. I do not love him."

"You care for him, which is more than I did the king when first we wed." She looks down at her gown, recalling something. "That first night, they fixed my night clothes and helped me to the bedchamber, but once the door was closed I threw something at him and he slipped away till morning when they came to parade us around at court."

"Why did you throw something at the king?"

"He told me I looked sour and I had best sweeten up or he would dunk me in a vat of honey. Oh, he riled me and I riled him back until I threw a basin of water at his head and he went to go find better company."

She lifts her eyes to me, repentant and wiser. "I could have been a better wife, and perhaps he could have been more tender, more persuasive to a frightened bride. All in all, I hope your wedding night is better than mine was."

"But I am not convinced that we should wed. I do care for your son, but my heart was given to another. I no longer have it in my possession."

"And Edmund knows this threat exists?"

"Yes—he says it is forgotten."

"And is it?"

"All but. It sits between us and there is a great hole where there once was comradeship. I feel at a loss. I cannot marry him; neither can I not marry him."

"And this other man, whom you have given your heart to, where is he? What has he to say?"

I shake my head in shame. "He doesn't remember me."

She gives her head a sad nod. "Then you must choose. Edmund deserves your decision. He has been good to you."

"I know, Your Majesty, I have much for which to be grateful—"

"Hush, child. No one despises you for your indecision, no one thinks you ungrateful. As one who has lived with regret over many years, I caution you to take this decision to heart and resolve within yourself what you will do."

"Yes, Your Majesty."

She squeezes my shoulder in an embrace and then leaves me in the quiet.

I whisper what I have heard the priests praying, knowing as I pray that I have been given my answer. I look up at the fresco, seeing the happy face of the Christ-child and smile back. Has this God answered my prayers?

Perhaps he has, though the task before me still looms.

I FIND Edmund in the library, a solitary room with the need of one large fireplace. It boasts three large shelves filled with books, a bench, and a table seated in the center of the room. There the prince is bent over, studying the genealogy of his lands. I close the heavy door without sound but he senses me near him and looks up in anticipation. I walk toward him, my hands in front of me trying to hold myself together.

"What can I do for you?" He smiles.

"Not marry me." The words are spoken, I try to breathe.

His smile has died a twisted death, leaving a cynical line behind. "You have found some way to reverse her curse and leave me?"

"Whose curse?"

He rises to confront me. "Your witch's. You have defeated me and will now reclaim your love."

"My beloved cannot remember me. I am leaving you because I do not love you."

"You don't have to love me to marry me. You will grow

to love me." His eyes are desperate as he reaches for me, holds me by my forearms. "You will love me in time."

"No, I won't. I will always wonder what else I could have done to undo the witch's spell. I will not make a good wife for you if I am pining away for another man. I must leave you to be honest with myself, though I will miss you. You have been so good to me—but I just can't." Tears trickle down my face.

He stares at me, his hands clinging to my arms. "I wish you to forget this and marry me."

I stare back at him, mesmerized, unable to fight his compulsion. I will marry him.

THE WISH

I rise from my bed viewing my chamber with fresh eyes. Directly across from my massive bed there has been placed a great silver rectangle, a wedding present from my prince. In the middle of the night, the servants brought it to me, so that the first thing I see when I awake is my image.

It is very strange to see myself fully for the first time. Without thinking to hide my hair, I approach the mirror like a child, excited, scared, in awe. Inside the object is a girl—in fact, a young woman—with clear, creamy skin, rosy cheeks, and a mass of golden curls reaching her shoulders. Her eyes, separated by an adorable nose, are green, emerald green, surrounded by a fan of golden lashes. Her heart-shaped mouth has pink lips, and her teeth are quite straight and white. Her figure, even in a formless chemise, is quite good, strong with slight curves. The girl in the reflection is me, and I am beautiful. I am embarrassed to think about it, but I seem flawless.

After the initial pleasure of seeing myself, my head

wilts like the flowers Edmund brings me day after day; this is why Edmund wants me, because of this girl in the reflection. He does not want me—he wants her. But I am her, part of me argues. For now, the other part concedes, but there will come a day when my smile will dim, my teeth will yellow and fall out. All too soon my face, neck, and hands will all bunch with wrinkles, and my complexion will become spotty. Will he be able to see my beauty then, or will he think of what I once was and cast me aside?

My thoughts spin and flee; I can only remember having felt unsettled for a moment. I must be ready, for he will come to visit me soon to see how I have enjoyed this latest present. We have much to do to prepare for the wedding, and though at first I did not enjoy the idea, I have grown ecstatic about it and spend all my days working on details. Anytime my mind strays and begins to think less happy thoughts, they come to an abrupt stop. I return to the joyous chore of preparing to marry Edmund, to be the wife he wants and needs. Nothing could fill me as this does.

I dress quickly and before I have finished covering my hair, Edmund is standing behind me, arms around my middle, kissing my neck.

"Do you like it?" he whispers, gazing at the woman in the mirror.

I stare into his reflected eyes and waver for a moment. I push aside my misgivings, mere tremblings of a nervous bride-to-be, I think. "Yes, I do. I have never seen myself full-out before, just caught glimpses from time to time."

"I thought not." He steps back and turns me to see him. "You have not the vanity that many a woman at court has. I wanted you to see yourself before the rest of them arrive so that you could see that you are not just superior in your mind and actions, but in your appearance as well. You are fit to be a queen, my Rapunzel."

I blush at his words. "Wait—the rest of them? Who is coming?"

"Most of the nobles from throughout the land will arrive starting today. It is the harvest. Have you not heard the bustle of the servants as they are hard-pressed to get ready for such a large arrival?"

I frown; I have been too preoccupied, it seems, to notice anything. But this should be something I take notice of; after all, it has to do with our wedding.

"No matter, you have been busy, and you need not worry. After all, you have met most of them already on our journey throughout the kingdom this summer."

I straighten my back; it will be a pleasure to greet the king's nobles. I follow Edmund out of the room and break fast while waiting for the first of the visitors to arrive.

BEATRIX HAS LEFT her chestnut hair loose, long, straight, and shining. Her dark eyes are bright with excitement, and today her figure is draped in luxurious shades of blue. As we greet one another, I notice her looking at Edmund for a moment too long and then smiling with almost a sneer as she takes my hands. I look for Gwynndolen and see that she is not accompanying her mother or two older brothers.

Her ladyship greets me with a kiss and moves onto the king and queen, leaving Beatrix to speak for the family. "I am sure you will be very happy in your coming marriage, my lady. Gwynndolen asked that I apologize for her absence. She could not come, as she is caring for our father so mother can attend."

I would have thought such a responsibility would have fallen to the oldest daughter, but I know that Beatrix is of age and would not miss a chance to meet eligible men—and make eyes at those who are already betrothed. Perhaps this last thought is beneath me, but I don't stop from thinking it as I eye her.

⊂⊇⊆⊃

I WAS TRAVELING through my dreams last night when I found a young woman. She looked like me, but sad. She soaked in a puddle of light and I wondered who she was. How did she come to be there? I could not touch her, for when I reached out, her image rippled like a wave. When I brought my hand back, it was wet. I was overwhelmed with sadness at seeing her, but the dream shifted and tried to pull me from her. I felt the need to free her, to release her from her watery prison. But all of a sudden, I was awake, and now I can remember no more than this. I feel her nearness even as I dress. I try to shake it off, but my mind is preoccupied with her predicament as though she is real and not a dream. What should I have done to help her?

⊂⊇⊆⊃

THE HARVEST WILL BE complete in two days' time, after which the festivities will begin—ending, of course, with our wedding. Edmund has promised that even the gentry will be included in some of the peasants' harvest games this year, due only to the fact of our being wed and ending the season with a much larger feast than the peasants of this generation have seen. I smile at this, for I miss games. I have fond memories of having played them long ago as a child, but I can't quite remember with whom or what the rules were. Everything but the wedding is a blur to me.

"Have you decided which of the surcoats you will wear tomorrow evening?" The queen smiles and takes my hands in hers as we meet in her sitting room.

"I have chosen the pale green." I return her smile.

"Which will look lovely when girded with this." She goes to her seat and picks up a cushion beneath which she has hidden a belt of garnets.

"My queen, you are too generous! These are so beautiful, so clear!" I stare into the depths of the dark red stones lying in my hands.

"They will not compare to the beauty you will radiate tomorrow night." She sighs with joy, clasping her hands together like a little girl. "To think—at the end of spring I was lonely atop my tower, relying on God's grace to carry me through. Now, I rely on His grace to keep me from clinging too hard to any of my daily miracles, the love of my husband, the return of my son, and the addition of a new daughter. In truth, I am blessed, Rapunzel. Who could be more so?"

I love to see the queen looking so happy.

"Now, daughter, how will you wear your hair? Down, I suppose, as the tradition of brides?"

"I'm not sure that would be appropriate, given its state." I unwrap my head and shake out the curls.

"Why your hair is very pretty, my dear, though rather short. Were you ill last year? I know of an apothecary who ordered every maiden to cut her hair during the plague to try to ward off the fever in the summer."

"Your Majesty, I am at a loss as to why it is so short. I feel certain it was very long, but I cannot remember how it came to be shortened."

"Ah—a mystery! Well, don't be disturbed, dear one, it was likely a fever. Many people remember little about the time they were ill."

"But I don't remember being ill."

"Well, that is curious."

I try to drop the subject and move onto something else, the wedding perhaps, but I feel the obscurity of my hair to be quite important, and possibly dangerous. "Will you help me wrap it back up?" I hear myself asking. "I think I will wear it plaited with ribbons and that should mask things."

Tomorrow, tomorrow, I hear the room whisper tonight. Tomorrow, tomorrow. I open my eyes, speculating where the voice is coming from. Tomorrow, tomorrow. But I can't see anyone. I feel exhausted and giddy; all the details and orders have been arranged. Now it is time only to wait and see what comes. Tomorrow, tomorrow. It almost sounds like a melodious song, someone serenading me on the night before my wedding. Someone wishing me charming dreams as I close my eyes . . .

. . . She is crying now, great drops of tears dripping from her lily-white face. She has been crying for a long time, for I can see how red her eyes are, how slumped her posture. Her breathing is irregular, punctuated by gasping sobs. "Why?" the girl asks, "Why am I such a fool?"

I step towards her once again. "My lady?"

She seems to have heard me and turns her large green eyes on me. "Can you answer the question?"

I know not of what riddle she speaks, but I feel certain that I must solve it. "I would like to try."

"Why am I lost? Why have I been forgotten?"

Her question makes me uncomfortable. I look around me, but all is dark, and I cannot see anything in the darkness but her floating image. "Do you know where you are?"

"I am here in this obelisque, where those waiting are forgotten, but not powerless."

"Who has forgotten you?" My voice quivers as I ask.

"You have. You have forgotten me, your true self, and instead allow yourself to be controlled by a wish."

I feel my face fall. There is truth here in this dream, but as I reach forward to grasp it, the dream is taken from me. Edmund sits next to me on my bed.

"Edmund!"

"My love! You are dazzling in the morning." He leans down to kiss me, but I push him away.

"What are you doing here? You must leave now or all of the servants will think—why, they'll think—"

"We have shared sleeping quarters before." His smile is teasing, but I don't understand.

"What? Have we? Surely not! Leave now or—or—"

"Or what?" He leans in and kisses the tip of my nose before I bat him away. "You have nothing to threaten me with, my dear, and tonight you will be my wife."

"Well, then, tonight you may bed me, but today you must away!" And I shoo him out, shutting the door, quite out of breath.

I look around the bedchamber and feel as though I must have been doing something, thinking of something important, but I cannot remember, so I ready myself to start the day.

ONE EAR of corn remains in all the fields we are to hunt. The men hide among the empty stalks and the maidens must venture forth to find the ear. Each must quietly try to retrieve it and get out of the cornfields before being captured. If she does not succeed, she will have to grant a favor to her captor. This is not the sort of game I have ever played, and I am not sure whether I like the idea of it or not. Of course, Edmund assures me it is safe as he has arranged for only members of the court to use one cornfield.

The older generation believes this is a ridiculous pastime for noble-born young people, but Edmund says we grew up differently from the others. We have longed to be outside, even in the heat of harvest, doing our share. Last evening, we snuck away from the castle so that he could play his lute for the workers. Not surprisingly, they were most appreciative. He seemed more himself then, and I felt more like I knew him. For a moment, I felt—

Well, no matter. I have noticed all of the young women and men who have come to celebrate the wedding of the prince are quite entranced by this idea of hiding and flirting. I hope Edmund is right and all will go well.

I break my fast as usual with the other women, questioning again how so many noble-born men go without food until midday. I would think gorging in the middle of the day because you have starved yourself does not make one exempt from the sin of gluttony. Oh well. I enjoy the company of Queen Lefwenna while I eat my porridge and pears, and we smile over the day to come. I thought my mind would be preoccupied with thoughts of each detail of this day, but instead, I seem to be floating on an air of impatient excitement.

Like most of the other nobles, the younger generation has been polite to me, but none has extended their hand in friendship. I notice again how they look at me while I eat, how I am not included in their set as they gossip, and I decide I can bear this. After all, my childhood was different from theirs, though I remember little of it. I know I was not born to this and I did not grow as they did. I detest the way Beatrix gazes at me, as though she knows I do not fit and that Edmund would be better off with another. Perhaps she is right—but he has chosen me. A queen must allow people to think what they will. I return my thoughts to my meal and decide the rest must be left alone.

THE FIELD HAS a deserted look to it. Nearly every stalk has been harvested, and only one of us maidens will find what has been left behind. I chose a dark green surcoat and brown cotehardie to try to blend as best as I can in the field, but I know that Edmund and the rest will be hard at work trying to find us. Though I have not made friends among the other maidens, I enjoy their excitement, their giggles, and, yes, their wispy looks of rapture as they whisper about my marriage. Beatrix alone disturbs me a bit, but her jealousy is misplaced. I sense she covets my position, not Edmund. If she but knew how he came by my hand—

I shake my head and sway but feel the wave of vertigo

pass in a moment's time. I see a servant reading from a scroll the rules of the adventure before us. I determine I will be the one to capture the final husk of corn and run out of the field before being captured. Edmund can capture me tonight, but not now!

The servant blows into a long trumpet from which stream King Purnell's colors of yellow and black. Off we run, trying not to giggle, a mad rush of females through the cornfields. I am quick and I manage to head in toward the center of the cornfield. I cut through several rows, away from the other girls and from where I believe the men are hiding to ambush them.

The stalks are quite tall, taller than I remember them being last night as I sat on the back of a wagon and listened to Edmund sing and play. Of course, I was not standing next to the stalks then, nor was I paying enough attention to how the peasants managed to get all the corn off of a stalk. I now see how difficult it will be to accomplish this task and remain silent.

The first scream is followed by loud giggles, and I shudder and then laugh at myself. I have managed to look over several stalks, top to bottom, by getting up on my tiptoes. I remained soundless by not touching anything. It's obvious now I will need to work a bit faster, as the first scream is followed at once by two more. I feel flighty as I hear another scream followed by capricious laughter.

As I step through to another row, I am caught by a young man with sandy brown hair and hazel eyes. He looks familiar to me, and yet foreign. I start to shriek as he reaches for me, but he puts his firm hand over my mouth.

Again, I am struck by how well-known that hand seems with its blunt fingers.

"Rapunzel—it's me."

I look at him like one who is dumb. This is not how the game is played. I don't even remember seeing this man in court, though he sounds foreign and his head might have been covered. Besides, there have been a great many of them arriving daily. I suppose—

No. I remember him, but not from here, from somewhere else. My mind seems stuck, and I remain mired as he removes his hand from my face. There is more here than a game, but I try to lighten the mood. I clear my face of expression and ask, "You have caught me, what favor do you wish?"

Now he is the one to look puzzled. "I am not here to play this game; I knew it was the one way to let you know I have come for you. I remember you, Rapunzel. I remember us."

I look around, feeling danger, unsure of how to respond to this strange and mystifying individual. Come for me? Remember me? "Sir, if you are not here to play our game, then you must let me go." His hands now hold my own, but ever so softly. "You see, my betrothed is determined to catch me before I get the last of the corn."

"Rapunzel" —he speaks as though I have misunderstood him—"I remember our plans. I have come to marry you."

"That you cannot, for I am to marry another at dawn." I try to laugh, perhaps this is part of the game. But no, his eyes are so intense, full of sorrow, pleading for me to listen, to understand.

"When you wept, I began to remember, just little pieces at first—but then, a week ago, it all came together, as though I had been blind, but my eyes are now clear. I had forgotten who I was, who you were, but now I remember everything."

"Sir, I know not of what you—" But I do know something, and though I could pull away, I don't. Something about him makes me struggle within myself, makes me fight the urge to slip back into my happy delirium of the past weeks.

We hear one, then two more screams, and I hear Edmund's voice approaching on my right side, a few rows away. "Rapunzel, we have caught all the others. I am coming to find you. You must give me a favor!"

The young man leans his head down and meets my eyes, not letting me turn away. "Come with me now. This is the one favor I ask of you."

I am running behind him until we reach a nearby clump of trees, not an orchard, but a piece of land that has never been cleared. As soon as the light dims and we can no longer see the way behind us, he turns and pulls me to himself.

I have come with him, holding his hand, fighting the urge to cry out to be rescued. I'm fighting it because something within me says that I am being rescued.

"Rapunzel, you came!" He smiles at me, his lips parting in a smile. He leans down to kiss me, but I pull back, scared.

"Who are you?"

"Your betrothed, Paul."

"How can that be?"

"We were separated by a witch. Your tears are a powerful potion. Though it took a few weeks, the memory of our love has returned to me and I have come to marry you." He smiles in triumph. "I have come to take you home to my father's kingdom."

I shake my head; his words are gibberish to me. "A witch? What witch?"

"Your guardian . . . Why can you not remember? Has the witch returned to curse you again?"

I shake my head, feeling fragmented and small. It is as though pieces of me are flying about, but I can't quite catch and assemble them. "A wish."

"A wish?"

"The girl in my dream said—" I shut my eyes to try to recall. "She said I forgot myself for a wish." But whose wish, and why? I stare hard at the man before me, attractive, inviting, I feel safe with him, but—

"Rapunzel!" I hear Edmund's voice, and I step backward, my hands slipping away from the familiar stranger.

"He's coming to find me." I look up from the ground. "I'm to marry him tonight . . . I told him—I told him I couldn't, that I was leaving—"

"Rapunzel?" The voice is nearer, laughing as though I am hiding in jest.

"He wished me to marry him, and I would have."

"I am your love." The stranger holds still, as though I am an animal he must not frighten away.

I step towards him and lift my head. He leans down, brushes his lips gently against mine, and I feel as though I am falling. Everything returns, bringing with it all of the emotions I have ever felt. My beloved holds me tight as I cry and laugh. He continues to hold on, for I have lost all my strength in recognizing where I am, who I am.

The trees around us begin to bend as a sudden wind comes. Edmund breaks through the entrance of trees and locates us, fury tightening his features.

"Unhand my betrothed!" he roars, his face an unnatural red.

My love pushes me behind him. "She was mine before you met her."

"But she is mine now—I have wished it." The two men unsheath their swords, and I back away further into the trees. The wind continues to blow, now howling, and I feel terrified at its might.

Abruptly, the wind stops and my tingling skin feels damp and cool. All becomes dark around me but for the shape-shifting creature standing caged before my eyes, the witch in all her darkness. "Is this what you longed for? To be fought over by two handsome princes? A dream come true, preposterous daughter! I thought I raised you to have more sense."

I recognize her voice, her teeth, but her form is bizarre to me. As she shifts appearances I see in her the old hag I knew as a child, then the peasant who walked beside me on my way to help Adeliza, and then she is the beautiful child she once was long ago, dark curls next to ivory skin. "Who are you?" I whisper, knowing she is my witch, but also that I do not know everything about her.

Her form changes again. She stands erect, long black hair unbound, curling, cascading down her back. Her forehead is fashionably high, her face an oval, with a beautiful mouth holding straight, white teeth. She is wearing a simple gown of dove grey, tight around the waist and then flowing out into a loose skirt, the sleeves wide around her wrists. She holds an elegant hand to her pink mouth, and I keep thinking that her green eyes remind me of someone. She puts her hand down. "I am who you have always imagined me to be: your witch, your best friend, your worst enemy."

"Why?" In my question is everything I've ever longed to know, but I cannot voice each question. I need to know: why?

"Your stupid mother"—a flick of her wrist and Cat stands between us, half in and half out of the cage, held still by two of the bars—"had everything she ever wished for but she wanted more. She wanted everything I had as well." She bends down to stroke the quiet creature. "You should have known better, Katterina."

My feline mother sniffs the air once and then speaks into the light haloing my witch.

"A sister does not expect treachery from her sister."

"You stole my love!" My witch is crying, her emotions raw, bleeding out.

My mother shivers twice, beginning her transformation. "I did not steal your love—he chose me."

"He was mine!" Her eyes, depleting their water, begin to reduce themselves to the glassy marbles I've always known them to be.

"He was never yours." Cat's human hand reaches past the bars to me. "She was never yours."

My witch's hair whitens and dulls. "You left me nothing."

"You left to become . . . this." My mother and I stare as

the witch becomes in appearance what I knew her to be, withered, but for her beautiful teeth.

"This is all that was left me. I had to escape the cruelty of man. He was not the only one who rejected me, you hated me! You hated me!" Her voice is a squeal.

"I didn't hate you. I just didn't love you as I should have. I was wrong. We were wrong to have hurt you. Forgive us."

Like a lake of ice breaking, my witch shatters into a thousand pieces, her wail going on and on. I clap my hands over my ears; I cannot shut out her horrible noise. The cage dissolves, releasing my mother, who walks around, recovering pieces her sister has left behind. She cries into the howl as her hands sort through the pieces, "Please, please forgive me! You must forgive me!"

"No!" The howl continues but stops as my mother holds up the one unbroken piece left behind, a frozen heart.

My mother takes the heart in her hands and holds it to her own. "Forgive me," she whispers.

Darkness covers everything at that moment, and I fall to my knees, using my hands out before me to try to feel my way around. "Mother?" I whisper.

"Rapunzel, I'm here. What are you doing on the ground?"

"I can't see, Mother, where are you?"

"I'm right here." I feel her lifting me by the hand, but still, I see nothing. She lifts her hand to my face and then touches my eyes. My abrupt blindness ends.

I look at her and I see our similarities. There is no darkness; I am surrounded by a multitude of thick trees stretching high into the sky where the day's sun filters through. My mother stands before me, her appearance regal, her green eyes, human.

"Poor child, you must open your eyes and see what has always been."

Over her shoulder there are two young men about to fight for honor; neither sees us until I walk towards them.

With confidence, I end it. "I cannot be yours, Edmund. I never was." The prince seems to deflate and I wonder why he tried so diligently to keep me. He will have to find someone else to remind him of the pink he lost. "There are many beautiful girls at court who would like to be caught. You will not need to wish them into subservience. Leave me, now."

"But I need you."

I look at him. "You need to find a way to become the man you want to be without me. Return to your court; your parents are waiting."

I think he is going to argue, so he surprises me when he doesn't. He looks at Paul and puts away his sword. He opens his mouth, then shuts it. He turns his back on me and walks away as though he has to obey my wish. Of course, I know that everyone has a choice. My life is proof.

I stare at Paul, whom I longed for, said goodbye to in the Dark Wood, even sought though he could not remember me.

"What do you wish?" His voice is husky with humility.

"To choose you."

He smiles. "Is it as easy as that? We can marry and live as one now?"

My mother smiles at me, tears running down her face,

her hands still holding the frozen heart. "You are free now to choose, Rapunzel. My greed and my sister's greed will no longer bind you."

I turn to the woman who gave me life and I kiss her. I want to follow the example of Queen Lefwenna. "I forgive you, Mother."

My love wraps me in his arms, and he tells me of his father's kingdom across the Illyan Sea in the Northlands where we will return with my mother. There we will begin our new life together. What will happen once we arrive? I do not know, but I will take each step carefully and learn as I go.

⚬⚭⚬

Want more now?

"She cannot begin at the beginning," my cat purrs. "She was not there at the beginning."

Would you like to begin at the beginning?

As my gift to you, I would like to send you a copy of the novella *Before the Tower* so you might see for yourself the story of two sisters, their struggle to survive, and their choices that led Rapunzel to life imprisoned in a tower. Get it here: dl.bookfunnel.com/wftepfzx96

There is darkness all around me except for a sword of light that breaks through the inky blackness. A voice rasps, "Why? Why did you leave me?"

The witch's withered frame steps into that single path of light.

"But you're gone. You couldn't forgive, and now you are no more."

Her cackle begins deep in her chest. "Am I really gone? There are many of us left, lurking in places you can't imagine. You try to snuff us out and we will grow stronger."

Appearing in midair, there appear three women speaking in strange tongues. My witch looks over her shoulders at them. They shimmer as she used to. They change appearance: one becomes a dragon, another one a centaur, and the last a leviathan.

"You see? I am not alone. There are others who are more powerful than even I."

My throat swells with regret. "I didn't want you to die."

"You wanted me to change, to stop being who I was. I'd rather die."

"And you did." How can I miss her, this woman who once imprisoned me? She separated me from my love, set me on a twisted path of painful discovery? I find, though, that I do miss her. I reach out with one hand, but she recoils in hatred.

"Get away from me! Death is better than life with a traitor like you!" She screeches and the scream goes on and on. I watch her break, leaving behind only her shattered, frozen heart.

"Rapunzel!"

My eyes pop open. My mother has her hand on my brow. I am lying on a cot in a cramped, dim room as the ground tilts from side to side. In time, my mind recognizes where I am—on a ship heading towards the Northlands to meet the family of my betrothed, Paul.

The nightmare begins to fade as I sit up. "Did I cry out?"

My mother's face creases in worry. "Not as loudly as last night." She asks me no questions of the darkness that still touches me at night. I could speak of it, but I don't want to. I push back the covers and begin to ready myself for the day. The captain said we should reach shore soon and I cannot still the anxiety that crowds my stomach.

GLOSSARY

Chemise: a slip-like gown that was worn as the first layer of dress for women in Rapunzel's world. It would be naturally colored, typically an off-white color. Often, this was worn as a nightgown when the other layers of dress would be removed.

Cotehardie: a fitted gown worn over the chemise with sleeves cut to various lengths according to station in Rapunzel's world. The higher the station, the more intricate the sleeves, sometimes tight at the elbows and bell-shaped at the wrist or short at the elbows with a streaming tail called a tippet. The bottom of the cotehardie might also be lined with fur to show off the station of a woman.

Inner bailey: another term for a castle's inner courtyard within defensive walls.

Nethersocks: stockings that were held up by garters above a woman's knees in Rapunzel's world.

Pillbox hat: a box-like crown worn by some married women of high station on the island of Rona in Rapunzel's world. Often, the wimple's ends were drawn over it.

Surcoat: the outermost layer of dress a woman would wear in Rapunzel's world, though she would wear a cloak over all in cool weather. The gown was sideless and would complement the cotehardie's coloring, often cut a bit short if the cotehardie beneath had a fur-lined hem. The surcoat was frequently embellished with embroidery.

Wedge: a grouping of swans.

Wimple: a piece of delicate white linen wrapped beneath the neck and often worn by married women in Rapunzel's time to cover their hair.

1. As Rapunzel continues her journey, she encounters another person who was isolated for a large portion of her life. When Rapunzel meets Edmund's mother, she is struck by the woman's lack of bitterness and spirit of forgiveness. How was the queen able to forgive?
2. How does this affect the queen's relationship with her son? With her estranged husband?
3. Can you relate to the queen?
4. Peace is something Rapunzel longs for, but in the story she seems to find it only in those who have surrendered their lives to Christ. Jesus said, "Peace I leave with you; my peace I give to you. Not as the world gives do I give to you. Let not your hearts be troubled, neither let them be afraid."[1] Have you ever experienced this kind of peace?
5. In the story, peace is not experienced the entire

time by those who claim Christ. Are they still following, or does peace ebb and flow?

6. Rapunzel dreams at one point that Paul tells her that her heart is becoming hard and full of hatred. When we struggle with unforgiveness, bitterness grows and by its very nature, it corrodes our souls. In Ephesians 4:31, we are warned to put it away from us, as though we should treat like a flame that will burn us from the inside out. How do you see Rapunzel wrestle with this as the story continues?

7. Do you find yourself in a similar battle with bitterness because of an injustice in your own life? Do you have someone you can talk to that can help you process your anger so that you can forgive?

8. By the end of the novel, Rapunzel has unraveled the mystery of her own life and found a way to make a decisive choice. Is there a choice you are struggling with currently?

9. What do you think would help you determine what to do?

10. Do you believe Rapunzel completely forgives her mother and the witch?

11. Rapunzel says that she wants to trust in God, but she doesn't seem certain how to do so. What do you believe will happen with Rapunzel's faith after the last page?

---

1. *ESV*, John 14:27.

ACKNOWLEDGMENTS

Oh dear, where to begin?

Always with my Lord and Savior for the life He has blessed me with, thank You! May You receive all the praise.

Jeff, you are amazing though you deny it. I thank God for you! Katie, Sydney, and Caleb, you are the best readers I could ever hope for. Your support lifts me up.

Mom and Dad, I am forever blessed by your love. Margaret, thank you for loving us. Joy, I miss you. Jeanine and Jessica, my characters would be flat without you. Allison and Lora, I am so glad to love and be loved by you. Uncle Doug and Aunt Celia, being "adopted" by you has been the greatest gift for our family. Jennifer, your friendship and helping hand has enabled our family to thrive during this difficult season. Mike, Heather, Josh, Travis, and Sean, I'm so glad to broaden my reading and action scenes because of your influence.

Jody, you are a gift of a friend and editor. You make my stories better! Beth, it is a joy to work with you at Fit2B. Learning about physical dynamics is growing my understanding of Rapunzel's journey. I am incredibly blessed by Amie and Allison as you give me great feedback to help make Rapunzel shine.

Gwynn, your prayers keep me going—thank you for sticking with me all these years. Kelly and Rachel, Mom and Dad2, your love and prayers continue to strengthen me. I am so glad I get to be your third. And thank you for the coffee! Lauren, Heather, and Kevin, your laughter and friendship have renewed me time and again. I am glad the Lord has kept us close after all this time. Sara and Mandy, your wisdom and sarcasm inspire me to enjoy life. Erica, I have learned so much from you and I am blessed by your help in this "chronic" writing journey! Karen, Bree, Hollie, Beverly, Tracey, and Erin, I am so thankful for your friendship and prayers. Tiffani, Candice, Linda, and Ruth, thank you for your love and prayers and wisdom.

Finally, to my favorite readers Sara, Eva, Justin, Sophie, Emory, Phoebe, and Harrison. You are each precious to me and I love knowing we are on this journey together!

A lover of books and fairytales, JacQueline uses her faith and life experience with chronic pain/depression to discover new ways of telling old stories as well as her own. She lives in North Alabama with her amazing karate husband and three book-crazy children. She takes every opportunity to drink coffee while wearing dangly earrings and the color purple. Join her newsletter when you download your free copy of *Before the Tower* by visiting dl.bookfunnel.com/wftepfzx96.

Find JacQueline at AuthorJRoe.com, and you can also follow her on social media:

facebook.com/jacquelinevaughnroe

twitter.com/jacquelinevroe

instagram.com/jacquelinevaughnroe